"I am prepared to buy you a small house," said Lord Umber dramatically. "In fact, I know of one available immediately, in Richmond. Very pretty little place, it is, and I will make you a very generous allowance." He stood back, well pleased with his generosity, and pondered the stir Felicia would cause when he presented her to his friends.

Felicia's smile froze as she realized she had once again misunderstood her benefactor. With a cry of horror, she tried to free her hand, but was overwhelmed by Lord Umber's strength as he gathered her into his arms and pressed his mouth relentlessly down on hers.

"Oh! my little beauty," he whispered hoarsely in her ear, one hand exploring her body. "We shall deal famously together, you and I."

FELICIA

by

Leonora Blythe

FAWCETT CREST • NEW YORK

FELICIA

Published by Fawcett Crest Books,
a unit of CBS Publications,
the Consumer Publishing Division of CBS Inc.

ISBN: 0-449-23754-0

Printed in the United States of America

10 9 8 7 6 5 4 3 2 1

FOR TONY

with special thanks and affection to
Ben Ross

One

James, the young, gangling underfootman, snapped the last lock shut on Felicia's trunk and bent down to buckle the leather strap. "That'll be all then, Miss Felicia?" he inquired.

"Yes, James. Thank you," Felicia answered and wished she could spare a coin to give him. But her aunt had given her just enough money for the journey to Manchester and not a farthing more. The few guineas that Mrs. Ambel, the housekeeper, had pressed into her hand last night were already safely sewn into the hem of her drab traveling dress.

James sensed her discomfort and hastened to reassure her. "Now, don't you be fretting, miss," he said. "You is goin' to be all right, away from 'ere. Be careful though 'ow you go on the stagecoach and don't you be lettin' strange folk talk to you." His voice was brotherly. "But I'm sure Mrs. Ambel 'as already warned you of that."

"Indeed she has," Felicia said, "and you may be sure I will heed the advice."

"Well, I'll be takin' this trunk of yours downstairs, miss, and you just come when you're ready. I reckon Mr. Jennings will 'ave the cart round by the back door in a few minutes, and you know 'ow sulky 'e gets if 'e's kept waitin' long." James paused. "And . . . and, Miss Felicia, I just wanted to say good-bye and good-luck." He held out his hand awkwardly, and Felicia quickly took it in hers.

"Thank you, James. I shall miss your cheerful whistle in the mornings." She smiled warmly. "And you know how sorry I am that I shall not be here when you and Annie get married."

James released her hand and picked up her trunk. "Thank you, Miss Felicia, and just remember . . . be careful who you speak to."

Felicia took one last look around the attic bedroom that had been her refuge for the last five years. Now that the time had come for her to go the feeling of apprehension that had been building within her evaporated. A sense of freedom washed over her, leaving an exhilarating tingle to her body.

"Mama, Mama," she whispered, "I will be brave. I promise. I will try to remember how you suffered without complaining. I will not let you down. But, Mama, why did you have to die?" A tear threatened to trickle down her cheek, but she resolutely brushed it away.

To take her mind off her mother, Felicia checked her

reticule to make sure that the few pathetic pieces of bric-a-brac she had managed to retain were safe.

There was a tentative knock on the door, and in some surprise Felicia opened it. A look of astonishment spread across her face as she saw her cousin. "Hello, Wendy," she said quickly, "whatever are you doing up here?" Felicia noticed that the rims of Wendy's eyes were red as though she had been crying.

"Mama said you had gone," Wendy sniveled, "with . . . without saying good-bye to me." She put a small, fat fist to her eyes and wiped away the tears. "And . . . and . . . you promised you wouldn't forget."

"And I have not forgotten," Felicia said briskly. She tried to suppress the annoyance caused by her cousin's words. It seemed that Aunt Gweneth was determined to make her departure as difficult as possible. "You know you are not allowed up here, Wendy," she continued more gently. "Run along to your room, and I will join you in a few minutes."

"Cousin Felicia," Wendy blurted out. "I just wanted to say that I am sorry you are going. Really I am. And I am sorry for being so horrid to you. I am going to miss you so." She broke off, sobbing.

Felicia was puzzled by Wendy's attitude. In the five years she had been at Graystones, this was the first time Wendy had ever shown any remorse for her behavior. Knowing her cousin well, Felicia suspected an ulterior motive. However, her tone was coaxing as she replied: "You will soon forget me. As soon as you arrive in London and get caught up in all the preparations for your debut, you will not have time to think of much else."

"But . . . but . . . you don't understand," Wendy

wailed. "I will not have anyone to help me." The tears started down her fat cheeks again. "I need you with me."

"Come, come, Wendy," Felicia said with some irritation. "You must know that is impossible. Your mother is sending me away. It was she who found me the position as governess in Manchester. As for needing me, I am sure Aunt Gweneth will hire you a proper lady's maid once you arrive in London."

But Wendy was not easily placated. "It is all your fault. I know it is, for Mama would never send you away. You . . . you are far too useful to her . . . and me," Wendy sobbed. "You do not want to come to London for I expect you will be jealous of me . . . en . . . enjoying myself."

Felicia listened to Wendy in exasperated silence until she could not bear it any longer. "Pull yourself together, Wendy," she said bracingly. "I do not have the time to stand and listen to your self-pity. In fact, you have delayed me so much that I will have to bid you farewell here." She looked down at her cousin, and resisted the temptation to put her arm around the plump, shuddering shoulders. "Here, take this." She held out a finely embroidered handkerchief that her mother had given her for Christmas. "Blow your nose hard, for you know how that always stops you crying."

Wendy grabbed the delicate piece of linen and screwed it up into a tight ball. "You are an unfeeling beast," she sniffed and stamped a foot. "You don't care what happens to me . . ." She looked up at Felicia slyly, and the expression of disdain she saw on Felicia's face goaded her into saying, "I shall go and tell Mama not to let you go, for I can see now that that is the very thing you want."

"That is quite enough, *Cousin* Wendy. I do not have to tolerate your tantrums any more. Go to your mother, by all means, but there is nothing you can do to keep me here. I am free of you both." She flourished her shabby reticule at her cousin. "I have my stagecoach fare and a little more besides, and that is all I need to get away from here." Her eyes were glittering in her anger, and the look of distaste she bestowed on her cousin made Wendy wince. "Now, go," Felicia continued. "Go quickly, before I say or do something we both regret."

Wendy fled from the room, her loud, angry sobs echoing down the narrow hallway. Felicia stood for a few moments and wondered at her daring. "I really *am* free," she said to herself. "I am free and without fear." She hugged herself happily and danced a few steps around the room. She stopped when she reached the mirror. "Aunt Gweneth," she said solemnly, "I hope I never see you again in my life."

She picked up her reticule, which had fallen to the floor, and without a backward glance walked from her bedroom. She swiftly descended the attic stairs, being careful to avoid the loose floorboard that always creaked when trodden on, and quickly crossed the upstairs landing to the servants' wing. She could hear angry voices coming from her aunt's room as she started down the last flight of stairs.

Her heart was pounding as she hurried down, and she stopped only to draw breath when she arrived in the kitchen.

"I was just coming to fetch you," Mrs. Ambel said, looking quizzically at the heightened color in Felicia's cheeks. "My, my, we are in a 'urry to leave, aren't we?"

Felicia took a long, steadying breath before she answered. "Cousin Wendy delayed me," her voice was demure. "But I think I had better go quickly before my aunt demands to see me." She grinned wickedly at the housekeeper. "You see, I had a slight argument with dear Cousin Wendy."

Mrs. Ambel looked at Felicia in astonishment. "Well, whoever would 'ave thought you capable of such a thing," she said in admiring tones. "You're right, though, you'd best be off before the bell goes."

Mrs. Dauncey stepped forward and presented Felicia with a large hamper. " 'Ere you are, Miss Felicia. Just a little something to keep you from starving on the journey. I'm only sorry there's not more, but . . ." She shrugged her shoulders.

"Dear Mrs. Dauncey," Felicia said. "Thank you for your thoughtfulness. I am sure I will not be able to eat half of it." The hamper felt quite heavy, and Felicia knew it would be filled with the delightful delicacies that her aunt enjoyed. "I shall always remember your many kindnesses to Mama and myself." She leaned over and dropped a quick kiss on Mrs. Dauncey's face.

Biting back the tears that were once again threatening, Felicia followed Mrs. Ambel out of the kitchen to the waiting cart. They had just reached the courtyard, when the sound of a bell could be heard. Mrs. Ambel ignored it. "She can wait," she mumbled crossly. "Just for once, she can jolly well wait."

Annie and James were standing by the cart waiting to say their final good-byes. Mr. Jennings, the coachman, was standing by the horse's head, waiting for Felicia with ill-concealed impatience. Mrs. Ambel cut the farewells short by sending Annie to answer the summons of the bell. Felicia was thankful. She could feel her self-control slipping.

She watched James toss her trunk into the cart and waited for him to help her up. As soon as she was settled, Mr. Jennings swung himself up and jerked the horses to a fast trot. Felicia tugged on her bonnet strings, making certain they were tight, and sat up proudly. Mr. Jennings sniffed loudly to indicate his feelings at having to bother himself with such a menial chore. It was an embarrassment to him to have to use the cart, but Lady Ormstead had insisted on this mode of transport, refusing to let Felicia have the use of her crested barouche.

Felicia turned to wave a final good-bye to Mrs. Ambel and James as the cart rounded the bend in the long driveway. As much as she would miss her few friends at Graystones, she looked to the future with excitement, so she turned her back on the big house with a great sense of release. She did not notice her aunt standing in the window of her upstairs drawing room, nor did she see the sly look of satisfaction on her aunt's face.

Felicia had no difficulty obtaining a seat on the stagecoach. The two ostlers at the inn in Chepstow, where the coach picked up passengers, were very pleased to be able to help someone so young and pretty.

"Don't matter 'er clothes are drab," the younger stableboy said, smacking his lips. "She's a good lookin' bit o' muslin, no two ways about it."

Felicia was indeed beautiful, almost a replica of her mother. Tall and slender, her golden hair framed a face that was exquisite in its delicacy. Because of the excitement, her limpid eyes, normally a violet-blue, were an even deeper shade.

The older boy agreed, nodding his head vigorously but keeping his eyes firmly on Felicia.

The excitement she felt made her oblivious to the ostlers' close scrutiny, and she was totally unaware of the other passengers waiting for the coach. One of them, a thin young man with limp hair and a bulbous nose, watched the stableboys' ogling with amusement. It would be a pleasant indulgence to while away the long journey to Cheltenham talking to such a lovely girl. He was tempted to exchange his cheaper outside ticket for an seat inside, although he could ill afford the additional expense.

As the blast of a horn announced the arrival of the coach, the thin young man made up his mind. He sidled closer to Felicia and muttered in an insinuating undertone, "Jason Hobbs, at your service. I couldn't help noticing you was on your own, as it were, miss. What do you say we team up as far as Cheltenham, if you take my meaning?"

Felicia made no reply to Jason Hobbs's impertinent suggestion. Actually she hadn't even heard it, so intent was she on enjoying the warmth of the spring sunshine and savoring her anticipation of the journey. The thin young man shrugged his shoulders and turned away. A sulky expression on his face reflected the thoughts arising from the imagined slight: *Who is she anyway? A common drab giving herself airs, that's who. But no denying she's a looker. . . .*

The courtyard of the inn had suddenly come alive. The

two ostlers ran forward to hold the heads of the sweating horses until the coachman threw them the reins.

" 'E looks a little worse for wear this morning," the younger boy muttered to his companion, nodding toward the coachman. "Let's 'ope 'e reaches Cheltenham in one piece."

A couple of passengers alighted, shaking their heads at the drunken coachman. He had his back to them, taking another swig from a bottle, so he did not see their gestures. Neither did Felicia. She was anxiously watching her trunk being hoisted up.

Only after it had been firmly strapped down did she climb into the coach. The younger ostler was there to assist her, and she thanked him prettily as he handed her the hamper of food. There was only one other passenger inside, the thin young man having settled himself in an outside seat. A prim, elderly woman was sitting in the far corner of the coach, pressed up against the side as though all the seats were taken. Felicia smiled at her, but the only sign the old woman gave to acknowledge the invasion of her privacy was to pull her capuchin round her thin body more securely and tighten her hold on her valise.

Felicia sat down and smoothed the creases from the shabby brown walking dress, before unclasping the frogging which held her cloak together. She was acutely conscious of the dowdy picture she presented but had decided that she would wear only her oldest clothes for the long journey. Mrs. Ambel had told her she would be able to change into something more becoming when she reached Manchester.

"It's no point dirtying your new gowns before you

need," Mrs. Ambel had said. "We don't want you arriving at your new position looking all crumpled and disheveled." She had omitted to make mention of her fears for Felicia's safety on the journey, thinking that fewer men would take notice of a girl who looked shabby and wore ill-fitting clothes.

The coach started with a jerk. Felicia settled herself more comfortably on the hard seat and looked over at the old woman. She smiled ruefully as she realized that the woman was asleep, for she had been hoping to start a conversation with her. She had so many questions to ask. Instead she turned her attention to the passing countryside. She knew it would take at least two hours to reach Gloucester; the innkeeper in Chepstow had so informed her. However, she was to stay on this coach until Cheltenham, where she would pick up her connection for the Northern Line. Her interest in the monotonous scenery outside soon waned, and her thoughts wandered to the family she was to join in Manchester. Initially, Felicia had been surprised that her aunt had bothered to spend time looking for a post for her, until she realized that her aunt wanted her out of the way as quickly as possible after her mother's death. In all honesty, she was glad to be away from Graystones.

Felicia looked down at her hands ruefully. The long delicate fingers were reddened from washing her cousin's fine underwear. As careful as she had been to rub salving cream into her hands, she had been unable to prevent the chap marks. She hoped that her new mistress would not expect her to do similar work, for it would be nice to have smooth hands again.

She flexed her fingers as though she were playing a piano and smiled happily to herself. At least she would be able to play again, she thought, once she had worked away the stiffness.

Although unused to traveling, she was not at all perturbed by the swaying of the coach, and in a short time, she too fell asleep. The small frown that creased her forehead as she slept was the only indication that she felt any apprehension of the future.

The lurching of the coach did not awaken her, nor the worried exclamations of her companion. Her slumber was deep, for she had not had much rest in the last few weeks. She had nursed her mother almost twenty-fours a day in addition to the usual chores her aunt had assigned her.

The halt at Gloucester was brief, there being no passengers to pick up. Only one man got off, and his complaints about the coachman passed unnoticed amid the general bustle of changing the team. They were soon on the road again, and Felicia was barely aware of the stop they had just made.

The old woman was wide awake though. For, with a fresh team to handle, the coachman was becoming reckless. She sensed something would happen and so was better prepared than Felicia when the drunken coachman took a sharp bend too fast and lost control of his horses. He might have managed to avert total disaster had he had the road to himself, but an oncoming curricle was the final obstacle he could not avoid.

Felicia awoke to the frightened screams of the old woman and, as she turned her horrified gaze outside, she felt the coach roll alarmingly before crashing over onto the dirt road.

The outside passengers were able to scramble to safety, but Felicia and the old woman were trapped. As the coach came to rest, Felicia was flung out of her seat. She landed head first on the opposite side, which had suddenly become the floor of the overturned coach. As she fell, her head struck the wooden door frame, and she felt a sharp pain. Then blackness swept over her.

Clasping her walking stick firmly in one hand, the old woman started to pound on the door that was not wedged shut against the ground. The coachman was unharmed but the enormity of his carelessness and stupidity had shocked him into immobility. The frightened horses were still bucking in the shafts. The five outside passengers were of no help, for they were still picking themselves up. So it was the gentleman from the curricle and his tiger who took over the task of calming the horses; and it was the gentleman himself who responded to the cries for help coming from within the coach.

"Just a moment," he called in a well-modulated voice, gingerly picking his way through the debris.

"Help me out, young man," the old woman commanded angrily. "I do not know what the world is coming to. If it's not highwaymen one has to contend with on the road, then it's drunken coachmen."

Climbing up on the coach, the gentleman pushed open the heavy wooden door and peered into the dim interior. The old woman's rantings received only scant attention, but he was startled out of his languor by the beauty that lay insensible beside her.

"Well, come on," the old woman screeched. "Get me out of here before I lay this across your back." She shook her walking stick at him.

The gentleman bowed slightly with an air suggesting that this was all too boring for words. "Forgive me, ma'am," he said with a bemused smile. In all his seven and twenty years no one had ever addressed him quite so rudely. "I was thinking how we could remove your daughter without adding to the damage already done to her."

"That trollop is *not* my daughter," the old woman snapped. "So don't worry your head too much about her." She sniffed condescendingly. "By the looks of her, she is some serving wench, though Lord knows how she can afford to travel in such luxury. No doubt she's no better than she should be."

Amused, the gentleman raised an eyebrow at the venom in her voice and wondered if perchance the harridan's vitriol was motivated by a twinge of jealousy. Completely disregarding his elegantly tailored clothes, he lay down on his belly, across the side of the coach.

"Are you ready, madam?" he asked.

He was just about to reach in, when Jason Hobbs came over.

"Can I help, sir?" the thin young man inquired fawningly.

"Indeed you can," the gentleman answered. "While I hoist the old dragon out, you can hold onto my feet." The old woman stiffened at these words.

"What are you waiting for?" she demanded loudly, waving her arms in annoyance. "Get me out of here immediately."

The gentleman ignored her command as he continued his conversation with Jason. "And then there's a young girl inside who appears to have a concussion. If you could relieve my tiger," he nodded in the direction of the man who was holding the horses, "he can help me get her out."

"Right you are, sir," said Jason, smacking his lips lecherously and slapping the gentleman on the back, to the latter's enormous surprise. "But I can help you with her. No problem there." The thought of laying hands on such a lovely piece of womanhood stirred his blood, all the more because of his recent unsuccessful advances. "I'll be only too delighted."

"Do you know her, then?" the gentleman asked noting the intimate tone in which Jason spoke of the girl.

"Never clapped eyes on her afore—until Chepstow that is. But I have it for certain she's a right little goer," Jason confided maliciously, his bulbous nose quivering. He had half-convinced himself of the truth of his allegations.

The gentleman, annoyed by Jason's quivering nose and presumptuous bonhomie, turned his attention to the irate squawks coming from the old lady. "All right, madam," he said briskly. "Are you ready now?" He reached into the coach and then clasped his arms around the old woman. "Push with your feet now," he commanded, and with great ease lifted her out.

Looking like an ill-tempered monkey, she blinked in the sunlight and then emitted a shriek of outrage when the gentleman unceremoniously set her down on the side of the coach, with her capuchin and petticoats all in a tangle around her bony shins.

"I will crawl into the coach and see how the young lady does," the gentleman said, leaving Jason to help the old woman down off the coach. The gentleman was determined not to let Jason aid in the rescue of the young girl, for he had taken exception to his excessive familiarity, and what better way to put the lout in his place than by casually thwarting his obvious lust for the girl. (Not that he faulted him for his desire—indeed, she was of unsurpassing beauty—but the gentleman felt that discretion was the better part of desire.)

"If you can ask the coachman to take hold of his horses, I would prefer the help of my tiger," the gentleman continued, in rather preemptory tones.

Jason was visibly disappointed at the request, but he reluctantly helped the old woman down and set her on the ground before badgering the coachman into action. Within minutes, the nimble tiger was cheerfully scrambling up the side of the coach.

"Yer wanted me ter 'elp yer, m'lord?" he asked, peering down into the darkness.

"Ah! Timothy. Just the person I wanted. Do we, perchance, have a blanket in the curricle?"

"Aye," the tiger answered. "I'll go and fetch it right away. 'Ow do you plan on getting 'er up, Guv? Don't look as though she 'as moved." His eyes had adjusted to the dimness, and he could make out the forlorn figure of the girl.

"I'll secure the blanket about her, Timothy, and then we will lift her out." He paused as he took another look at Felicia. "Then I think we'll take her with us to Alverston, for I do not trust the motives of some of the passengers. She will be far safer there, and I know Dr. Ross is in residence. He'll be able to tend her." And, he thought to himself, she may well want to thank me for my kindness in saving her from her fellow passenger. He smiled to himself at the thought. She would make a nice interlude. "How is the coachman?" he continued.

"I reckon 'e's sobered up a bit now, but 'e's still shaky on 'is pins. I pity the passengers," the tiger added, "for it don't look like 'e's going to get 'elp in a 'urry."

"All the more reason to take the damsel with us, Timothy," the gentleman said. "I feel sure she is in immediate need of attention. Make certain you get her luggage before we go."

"Very good, m'lord," the tiger grinned. "I'll just go and get that blanket."

Jason watched anxiously as the two strangers lifted Felicia out of the coach, and he laid his coat on the ground as a pillow for her head. He was hoping they would be on their way once they had accomplished their task, for he wanted nothing more than to have Felicia to himself when she regained consciousness. He would present himself as her rescuer . . . she would be *so* grateful. . . .

The gentleman had been surprised by Felicia's frailty as he had wrapped her in the blanket. Her face was classically beautiful, and except for her drab clothes and worn hands which clearly indicated she was from the serving classes, he would have thought her a lady.

He laid her on the ground gently and then stood back and surveyed the other passengers. The old woman's lamentations were commanding the attention of everyone except Jason. He was hovering over the prone body of Felicia, leering at her suggestively.

He looked up at the gentleman. "My name is Hobbs, sir, Jason Hobbs," he said obsequiously.

The gentleman tipped his hat. Choosing one of his lesser titles, he answered, "Sir Ian Gordon."

"Well, thank you, sir," Jason said, only slightly taken aback, "for getting this pretty little miss out so quickly. Now, if only we can get the coachman to go for help, we will be all right."

Sir Ian looked at him with a disdain that belied his civil words and flicked an imaginary speck of dust from his corded sleeve. Increasingly he objected to the smirk that appeared on the man's face every time he looked at Felicia.

"I would not rely on that one to do anything," he said haughtily. "He will be pleased to know, though, that I intend relieving him of his greatest problem." He looked down at Felicia. "I will take this young lady with me."

Mr. Hobbs's bulbous nose reddened in frustration, and Sir Ian was reminded of a clown he had seen in Italy once—the whitened face and the nose painted crimson. Sir Ian smiled briefly to himself. Whatever his faults, he was honest, and he admitted to himself he was having a deuced good time putting this presumptuous lout in his place while making off with a gorgeous prize.

"But you cannot do that," Mr. Hobbs said angrily. "You do not even know the girl."

"Immaterial," Sir Ian said, with an airy wave of a gloved hand. "And as I can insure that she will get medical treatment immediately, I am certain she will be grateful for my help."

No longer obsequious, Jason glared at Sir Ian. "You gentry are all the same. Always think you know what's best for everyone."

"Enough of your ravings, young man," Sir Gordon said lightly. He signaled to Timothy. "Bring the curricle over, and let's get the lady on board."

The old woman looked over as she heard this command and started to complain loudly. "I told you," she said angrily to anyone who would listen. "Didn't I? He's only interested in the girl. He don't care one bit that I probably have a lasting injury." She clutched her side as though in pain. "Oh!" she moaned, "I hurt so badly, especially here." Her moans turned to loud yelps as she realized that no one was listening.

"Be it safe to move 'er, sir?" one man asked. His ruddy complexion and stocky build indicated that he was a farmer. "I mean, she ain't even moved a whisker."

Sir Ian was beginning to wish he had not involved himself in the whole affair. Nothing took the savor out of an escapade like complications.

"In the circumstances, I think it is the wisest thing to do," he said loftily. "It appears to me that the young lady has sustained a severe concussion, and when she comes round she will not appreciate finding herself stretched out on the highway."

Silenced by Sir Ian's air of having delivered a pronouncement of irreproachable logic, the group fell back and formed a path for Timothy who was approaching in the curricle. Sir Ian lifted Felicia in his arms and carefully placed her on the seat, then swung himself up and sat down beside her and placed one arm around her. Timothy handed him the reins and within seconds they had left the scene of the wrecked coach.

Sir Ian grinned ruefully. "I hope this sweet young thing appreciates what I have saved her from," he remarked. "A week with me is bound to be better than a lifetime with Mr. Jason Hobbs."

Timothy grinned knowingly. "A day, more like, Guv,"

he said cheekily. "Not a bad bit o' muslin, is she? Dressed up in a bit o' finery, and I reckon she'll look bonny."

"The trunk, Timothy," Sir Ian exclaimed. "We forgot her trunk!"

"Just as well, if you don't mind me saying so," Timothy responded. "By the looks of what she's wearing, t'other clothes won't be worth much."

Sir Ian nodded. "You are quite right, Timothy. It's certainly not worth returning to the coach to retrieve them." He chuckled to himself as he thought of the old woman's squawkings. "And I do not think I can face any more complaints."

Timothy laughed. "That ole lady would 'ave like to run you through with 'er cane, she would. Anyways, it gives 'er sommat to talk about to 'er friends."

Felicia started to slip in her seat as Sir Ian took a bend a little too fast. "Steady her, Timothy," he commanded. "I would hate for her to take another tumble before she recovers from the first."

Timothy leaned over and put his arms around Felicia's shoulders. He looked down and saw an ugly gash on her right temple. "Better spring the horses, Guv'," he said gruffly, "to the nearest village. I reckon a doctor ought to take a look at this cut. And t'will be best to get 'er into a bed fast."

Sir Ian glanced down at Felicia. "In that case, I will continue with my original plans."

"What, visit your mother?" Timothy gasped.

"Indeed," Sir Ian said airily. "Dr. Ross is staying there for a few days, and if this young lady has any lasting injury to her brain because of the crash, he is the one doctor in England who can help."

"But won't the dowager be insulted when she finds out that she 'as been asked to entertain one of your ladies?" Timothy asked nervously.

"If she knew, maybe she would," Sir Ian laughed, a devilish look in his blue eyes. "But as you and I are the only ones who know of my plans, I think we can get away with it this once."

Two

*Felicia opened her eyes and found her-*self staring into the unfamiliar face of a severe-looking gentleman who was bending over her. A deep frown drew his thick eyebrows together, making him look older than his twenty-eight years. She let out a frightened gasp and instinctively pulled the bedclothes up around her chin.

"Who . . . who . . . are you?" she asked warily.

The man straightened up, and his concerned expression vanished. He was pleased to see that Felicia's movements in bed were quite normal and not painful, for he had been uncertain whether or not she had sustained any fracture to her ribs.

"There, there," he soothed. "I am a doctor. You have been in an accident and have suffered a mild concussion." He patted her hand reassuringly, then continued as he saw her expression of dismay. "Don't worry, miss. Don't worry, for we will soon have you on your feet."

Felicia's feeling of dismay turned to bewilderment when she raised her hand to her head and her fingers encountered a bandage.

"Accident?" she queried feebly. "I do not seem to remember." She stared intently at the doctor's face for some sign of comfort. She struggled to think about what had happened, but her mind remained stubbornly blank, and she could not prevent the tears from rolling down her cheeks.

"There is no need to be frightened, my dear," the doctor said softly. "You are quite safe now."

"But you do not seem to understand," Felicia broke in, her voice trembling. "I cannot remember who I am." She shook her head as though to clear it and winced as a sharp pain stabbed behind her eye. She saw a gleam of interest light the doctor's face. Not understanding, she felt a panic deep within her. "What am I going to do?" she cried out.

Oblivious to her appeal, the doctor scrutinized her carefully. "That is very interesting," he murmured, "very interesting. You are fortunate, young lady, that I am here to tend you." He paused, as though conscious of his own importance. "Dr. Ross is my name. Dr. Paul Ross." He rocked slowly back and forth from his heels to his toes, his fingers tucked into the lapels of his ill-fitting old-fashioned jacket.

Felicia struggled to control her sobs. The doctor's voice was reassuring. "But . . . but . . . I do not understand what has happened to me," she whispered.

"Nothing that rest and a little treatment won't cure,"

Dr. Ross responded in kindly tones. "The stagecoach you were in crashed, and you were thrown about a bit. Must have hit your head on something sharp, for you have a nasty cut over your eye."

Felicia shook her head slowly and said with a slight shrug, "I do not recall anything. Who . . . who am I?"

"That is an easy one," Dr. Ross smiled. "See here, I found this letter in your reticule. It is a letter of introduction to a Mrs. Barton, in Manchester." He paused to see if there was any response to the name, then continued when Felicia shook her head. "And it seems that you are Felicia Richards, in your way to being governess to Mrs. Barton's two children."

"How strange that sounds," Felicia said with misgiving. "It means absolutely nothing to me. Oh! Dr. Ross, whatever am I going to do? I do not even know where I am."

Dr. Ross looked down at his patient and was impressed with the intelligence he saw in her face. The clear-cut features were a refreshing change from the aging, cantankerous patients he normally had to deal with. There was a freshness and innocence about her that he liked, and he was not immune to her blond loveliness.

He sat down on an uncomfortable, straight-backed chair that stood by the side of the bed. The sparsely furnished room was typical of a servant's room.

Felicia eyed him nervously, not liking the lengthy silence that had developed. "Please, please tell me what happened," she begged. "And where am I? There must be someone I should thank for helping me."

"My dear young lady," Dr. Ross said thoughtfully. "I will not deny that you are in a peculiar position." He held up his hand as Felicia started to say something. "No, wait a while for me to explain matters. You are at Alverston, Lord Umber's country seat."

"Lord Umber?" Felicia queried.

"To be more precise, the Earl of Alverston and Umber." He paused, allowing Felicia time to absorb this information, but seeing the puzzled expression still on her face he added, "Umber is the senior peerage. Be that as it may, he came upon the scene of the accident moments after it had happened and was responsible for pulling you and your traveling companion to safety." Dr. Ross smiled briefly to himself. He could well understand Lord Umber's impulsive offer to help Felicia, for it was well known that he could never resist a pretty face.

"I was traveling with someone?" Felicia asked hopefully.

"No, no, just sharing the inside of the coach. It was a mistake Lord Umber made, but the other lady soon put him to rights."

An unhappy sigh escaped Felicia as she realized there would be no help from that quarter.

"As you were unconscious," Dr. Ross continued, "Lord Umber decided to bring you here, knowing I was in residence and could possibly be of assistance." He looked away, as though in modesty at this seeming self-praise.

"You must think me incredibly stupid," Felicia said, "but I must confess that I cannot recall ever having heard your name before."

"As you cannot recall your own, I feel no insult about your lack of recognition of mine." Dr. Ross laughed and Felicia smiled hesitantly at the joke. "Anyway, your thanks should go to Lord Umber for rescuing you, and to his mother, the dowagar, for insisting that you stay until you have recovered sufficiently to resume your journey."

"But . . . but how long will it take for me to remember?" Felicia asked, determined to know the worst.

"It may take a few days or a few months. You must also face up the fact that it is entirely possible you will never regain your memory."

Felicia looked at Dr. Ross in horror. "Never! I could not bear it!" Her frail body shook with her effort to control herself. "Never to know who I really am! Oh! Please say that it cannot be so!"

Realizing that he had been too harsh, Dr. Ross attempted to calm her. "There, there. I only mentioned that as a possibility. But I have great faith in my ability to cure you." He smiled down at her with such cheerfulness that her fears vanished.

"What is this cure you speak of?" she inquired.

Dr. Ross hesitated. He always found it difficult to explain the method of treatment he had studied under Anton Mesmer. "It is somewhat of an experiment, really. You see, your amnesia could be caused by several factors, and I first have to ascertain whether they are emotional or organic. To do this, I will put you into a trance and ask you some questions."

"A trance?" Felicia queried, her natural intelligence making her take an interest despite her unhappiness. "What is a trance?"

"It is a sleeplike state during which you will appear to be unconscious, but you will be able to answer my questions. If the primary reasons for your amnesia are organic, you will be cured in a very short time. However . . . should they be emotional . . . I cannot even hazard a

guess . . ." He paused to suppress the excitement he felt.
". . . because you will be the first patient I have treated
for such amnesia." There, it was out—and he waited for
Felicia to complain.

Exhilaration surged through him as he realized that she
was not protesting. "But I cannot stay here," she pointed
out. "I cannot impose on the hospitality of strangers."

"You must not regard it so," Dr. Ross said emphatically. "In fact, you could be of great assistance to me.
The dowager is in sore need of a companion, and I will
suggest to her that you would suit admirably." There was
simply no way he was going to let this opportunity out of
his grasp. Indeed, his motives were not entirely selfish.
The dowager was in need of distraction, since most of her
illnesses were imagined, brought on by ennui. If, Dr. Ross
reasoned to himself, she had someone else to think
about, it was quite conceivable the lady's health would
improve.

"You are too kind, sir," Felicia said gravely. "But I do
not think I can accept such charity. You do not know
anything about me and, for all you know, the dowager
and I would not suit."

"Nonsense, my girl. Absolute nonsense. 'Tis not charity
I am proposing, but a good position that will pay well.
Now, excuse me while I go and make the arrangements."

He rose and was out of the room before Felicia could
object further. However, his enthusiasm was infectious,
and almost against her will Felicia felt a sense of optimism. There was no denying it would be quite unthinkable for her to go off to this Mrs. Barton in Manchester
knowing nothing about herself but that her name was Felicia Richards. She resolved to write to Mrs. Barton and

explain the predicament she found herself in. Maybe this information would persuade Mrs. Barton to keep the position open until she recovered. Having decided on this plan of action, she felt much better and even managed to smile at the consternation her letter would probably cause Mrs. Barton, whoever *she* was.

As he hurriedly descended the stairs, Dr. Ross was so elated at the opportunity to test his animal magnetism theories he didn't notice Lord Umber hovering on the upper landing. For his part, Lord Umber's attention was on the forthcoming encounter with the delectable morsel enscounced in the servants' quarters. He knocked lightly on the door and, after Felicia answered "Come in, please," he entered the shabby room.

His thoughts were interrupted by the sight of Felicia, who looked frail and winsome with the white bandage bound tightly around her blond head. She looked nothing like the governess she was pretending to be. The little minx.

"You must be Lord Umber," she said in a musical and slightly breathless voice, momentarily overawed by the magnificence of the handsome young man standing so tall and dark in the doorway. His fitted breeches seemed to be molded to his strong thighs, and his jacket, of pale blue superfine, was fitted to his gracefully muscular torso with all the skill his Saville Row tailor could command. With his classic features and dark curling hair, he was the most handsome man Felicia had ever seen. Except, she reminded herself, the only other man I can *remember* seeing is Dr. Ross. Felicia looked at him steadily. "You are correct in your presumption, Miss Richards," he drawled languidly, an expression of boredom in his eyes. "Although I sometimes use another title." He thought an explanation due, in case she had heard him introduce himself earlier as Sir Ian Gordon.

"I . . . I . . . do not know, m'lord. Has not Dr. Ross told you I have lost my memory?"

Lord Umber eyed her appreciatively. The bandage around her golden hair did not detract in the least from her beauty. He pulled himself together hastily as he realized Felicia was waiting for an answer. "No, I have not seen him since he visited with you, but you must not let the fact that you have lost your memory temporarily distress you." What a charming charade. An artful baggage, pretending to have lost her memory!

Felicia looked at him gratefully. His easy assurances bolstered her sagging spirits. "Your belief in Dr. Ross's abilities gives me great confidence," she replied. "But I cannot feel happy about presuming on your hospitality."

He liked her pretense at independence but quickly sought to bring her to the point. "Well, as to that, Miss Richards, I think I can set your mind to rest."

"Sir!" she gasped indignantly, as he moved over to the bed and took her hand. "Please, sir!" She tried to draw her hand away without seeming too rude.

"Don't be frightened," he said lightly. "I am not going to harm you." As though she were a child, he gently stroked her hand, which she had been unable to retrieve. "I have given some thought to your future, and methinks you will enjoy my solution." He was surprised to see a faint blush tinge her cheeks.

Felicia was thoroughly alarmed by now. Lord Umber no longer looked languid, but like a panther ready to pounce. The bored look in his eyes had been replaced by an avid gaze.

Lord Umber took her silence as feigned modesty. *Egad,* he thought, *I believe she wants to be wooed.* He chuckled to himself at the thought of the sport ahead. Her air of innocence only heightened his desire. She really was an original, like a delicate rosebud ready to burst into full bloom. Her lips had a provocative pout that barely concealed the obstinate set to her mouth that he had noted earlier. By God she was a tempting little thing!

He leaned closer and whispered in her ear, "My suggestion is quite simple, really. I want you to live under my protection."

Felicia relaxed slightly, totally misunderstanding the suggestion. She silently chided herself for her foolishness and gave him a hesitant smile. "Dr. Ross did mention that your mother was in need of a companion," she concurred, "but as I told him we may not suit. However, if you think . . ." Felicia broke off as she saw Lord Umber arch his brows in surprise.

"He did, did he?" Lord Umber said carelessly. "I wonder what gave him that notion, for I assure you, my dear Miss Richards, that position was not quite what I had in mind for you. No. I have something more worldly for you. Something I know you will enjoy."

"I cannot think what you mean," Felicia said, sniffling loudly in an effort to stem the tears that were forming in her eyes. His presence was becoming oppressive. She was very tired, her head ached, and she wished he would go.

Lord Umber was amused by Felicia's behavior, although her pose was growing a bit tiresome. The role of the innocent damsel she had adopted was enticing. He silently handed her his scented, lace handkerchief and watched as she blew her nose furiously.

"I am prepared to buy you a small house," he said dramatically, making the decision to negotiate openly with the girl. "In fact, I know of one available immediately, in Richmond. Very pretty little place, it is. I would staff it fully, of course, and . . . and . . ." he paused as he thought of what else he could offer, "and . . . and apart from kitting you out in the very latest style, I will make you a very generous allowance." He stood back, well pleased with his generosity, and pondered the stir Felicia would cause when he presented her to his friends.

Felicia's smile froze as she realized she had sadly misunderstood her benefactor. With a cry of indignation she snatched her hand away, only to be overwhelmed by Lord Umber's strength as he gathered her into his arms and pressed his mouth to hers.

"Oh! my little beauty," he whispered hoarsely in her ear, one hand exploring her body. "We shall deal famously together, you and I."

Hot anger swept over Felicia. How dare he take such liberties with her. With a strength born of fury, she twisted away from the bombardment of fervent kisses.

Lord Umber looked down and saw that her fists were clenched, the knuckles a livid white. He was an experienced lover, and it was all too obvious that this woman's reluctance was not feigned.

"How dare you, m'lord," she cried out, her eyes flashing furiously as she quickly pulled herself away. "Whatever have I done to deserve that?" She wiped the back of her hand across her mouth, as if trying to erase even the memory of his kisses.

"Don't tell me you have never been kissed afore!" Lord Umber said abashed, a horrible suspicion growing in his mind.

Felicia lowered her head in confusion. Her heart was still beating rapidly, and the sensations his hand had caused in her body were perplexing. Frightening, yet not distasteful. "I cannot answer that, m'lord," she said icily, "for I cannot remember. I can only tell you that I cannot recall ever having to endure such disrespect." She spoke instinctively, an inner knowledge telling her that Lord Umber was behaving disgracefully.

There was a quiet dignity about her that made Lord Umber pause. It occurred to him that Jason Hobbs and the old woman might easily have misled him, deliberately or not. No doubt of her being from the servant class, but her responses to his advances left him convinced she was a virgin. Somehow, this enhanced her appeal for him . . . the kisses he had just stolen had been like nectar. He was eager for more.

Felicia stared at him aghast, feeling ill-equipped to deal with her conflicting emotions.

"I beg you to leave me alone," she said quietly, her indignation made plain in her tone of voice. She felt shaken, as she recoiled instinctively from all Lord Umber's overtures.

He looked at her intently. "I do believe you are serious," he drawled, concealing beneath a vague smile the genuine surprise and embarrassment he felt at having forced himself on an innocent. "I am sorry to have offended you. I do hope you will forget my suggestion and consider Dr. Ross's proposal, for I have a feeling that you and mama will deal admirably together."

Before Felicia could decide whether to reply to his insultingly casual apology, he was gone, throwing her a careless wave as he closed the door behind him. She stared at the door in annoyance. She certainly had no intention of remaining at Alverston to be further subjected to his loutish importunities.

Her mind made up, she got out of bed and gingerly walked to the closet. Once she was dressed, she thought, it would be easy enough to slip downstairs and out of the house. Finding a stagecoach stop might be difficult, but if it meant walking five miles she would gladly do so, for she was determined to have nothing more to do with the arrogant earl.

Three

Felicia came upon an upstairs maid, who was polishing the already gleaming brass rail, as she left her room.

"Oh! Miss," the maid gasped, "you frightened me. I didn't think to see you up for a day or more."

Felicia smiled at her wanly. "I am sorry to have startled you," she said. "But I really feel much better now, and I think it best to be on my way."

"I dunno about that," the maid responded slowly, "for the doctor was most particular about me keeping an eye on you. And 'e's not a man what worries himself unduly."

"That is absurd, for I am feeling much better now. Really I am, as you can see," Felicia protested. "So please don't be concerned. I must be on my way, for I am undertaking a new position and I do not think my prospective mistress will look kindly on my tardy behavior."

39

The maid nodded in understanding. "I know what you mean," she agreed sympathetically. "It's so difficult nowadays to get anything 'alf-way decent."

Felicia smiled at her, thankful that she had the maid's understanding. "Then you must know how I feel," she confided. "I know Lord Umber and Dr. Ross are well-meaning, but they cannot possibly realize what it means to be out of work."

"You're so right, miss, but even so I think I should obey orders. Otherwise I will be out looking for work meself." The maid pulled a wry face and bobbed a curtsy.

Felicia was about to protest, but sensed the futility of it as the maid turned and ran down the stairs. Sullenly, Felicia returned to her room and sat down disconsolately. Her sense of frustration deepened as she realized the enormity of her situation. No money, no friends, no memory.

"I feel like a prisoner," she muttered to herself, "and the sooner I tell this Dr. Ross that I cannot possibly stay and help him, the better. For all I know, his intentions are the same as Lord Umber's, although he seemed honorable."

She turned quickly as a voice broke into her musings. "I beg your pardon," she said, as she looked up at Dr. Ross. "I did not hear you come in."

"Whatever has happened to overset you so?" Dr. Ross asked kindly. "I cannot allow a patient of mine to become so overwrought."

Felicia glanced at him impatiently. " 'Tis nothing, doctor," she replied hastily. "I have merely decided to waste no time in getting to Manchester and now find that I cannot leave because a maid has been told to watch me." She paused, waiting for Dr. Ross to explain his actions. He looked at her shrewdly, but said nothing. "Anyway," Felicia continued lamely, "it is wrong that I should impose myself on strangers, especially when I am expected elsewhere."

"I see," Dr. Ross said at last. "I am told that Lord Umber paid you a visit. Mayhap he said something that unnerved you? And I apologize for the maid," he continued, not waiting for a reply to his question, "but Lord Umber has a . . . a . . . reputation," he paused again, hesitant to express his real reason for wanting to protect Felicia, ". . . and . . . and I thought it best to leave you some protection, flimsy though it was."

Felicia felt a blush creep up her neck at his perceptiveness, but she managed to maintain her composure. "No, no, Lord Umber has said nothing to disturb me," she answered quickly, not understanding why she did not reveal what had really happened. "It is just that I know I would be happier away from here."

"Come, come, Miss Richards. I have known Lord Umber since we were in shorttails together, and if he has upset you, I beg you to forget it." Dr. Ross's voice was grave. "I cannot let you risk the possibility that you may never remember who you are, which is something you must face up to if you leave Alverston."

Felicia held back a sob. "That is too terrible to even contemplate," she whispered, "I . . ."

"Then my advice, Miss Richards, is to forget about whatever you and Lord Umber discussed. Underneath the veneer of irresponsibility, he is the kindest of men. I personally believe his father's death affected him more than even he realizes. The only worry you should bother about is your own well-being." Dr. Ross paused for a moment as he thought of Lord Umber. He had been devoted to his father, and to have actually witnessed him falling to his death six years earlier must have scarred the young man's mind. "You must let yourself be guided by me," Dr. Ross continued as he walked over to Felicia and patted her shoulder reassuringly. "It is all arranged for you to become Lady Louisa's companion. Indeed, she is most anxious for you to start your duties. And I will have a word with Lord Umber and insure that you are not bothered in the future."

Felicia looked at him in amazement. "I do not understand why you should bother with someone you have only just met. It surely cannot matter to you what becomes of me."

"Maybe you will understand one day, my dear, but for the moment, suffice it to say that my most important patient will benefit greatly from your presence."

"You are a very persuasive person, Doctor," Felicia laughed lightly, unshed tears sparkling on her lashes. "Maybe we can reach a compromise that will make everyone happy. I will stay here until we hear from Mrs. Barton. If I write to her today and explain my predicament, maybe she will keep the position open for me."

"My persuasive powers are obviously not enough to overcome your spirit of independence," Dr. Ross replied, a look of admiration lighting up his tired eyes. "However, I agree with your suggestion. If I am lucky, I will have had three weeks to treat you by the time those letters have been exchanged."

Felicia rose from the bed, "In that case," she said, "shall we begin?"

"My dear Miss Richards," a soft voice greeted Felicia as she entered the drawing room. "How kind of you to agree to stay."

Felicia looked toward the window and was amazed to see a delicate, almost ethereal-looking woman lying on a chaise longue. The light from the window fell in rippling patterns on the deep green chintz day dress she wore, which matched the color of her lively, dancing eyes. Her hair was dressed in the fashionable frizzed style, and small ringlets fell about her ears in seeming abandon. "I am Lord Umber's mother," the voice continued musically, "but I do hope that you will call me Lady Louisa, for I cannot bear the formality of being addressed as Lady Umber. And I shall call you Felicia." Lady Louisa's voice was soft and friendly, and Felicia felt an immediate liking for her new benefactress.

She advanced quickly to the chaise and dropped a deep curtsy. "I am indeed delighted to make your acquaintance, Lady Lousia," she murmured, gazing down at the exquisite oriental rug.

"Come, be seated, child," Lady Louisa said gaily, at the same time patting a comfortable chair that had been placed by the side of the chaise. "I want to know all about you. Oh! How silly of me—you don't remember, do you? I am sorry."

Felicia straightened slowly, giving herself time to adjust to these new surroundings. It seemed absurd that this young-looking woman could be the mother of the cynical man she had met earlier. "Not yet, ma'am," she answered, sensing Lady Lousia's concern. "But Dr. Ross assures me that it is just a matter of time before my memory returns."

"Well, in that case, we must talk about me and this cure the doctor has recommended," Lady Louisa paused and looked at Felicia closely. "You know, you are a fetching young lady," her voice was thoughtful as she continued, "despite that frightful gown you are wearing." The amusement in her eyes took the sting from her words.

Felicia laughed. "I must agree with you about the gown, ma'am. But it is the only one I have."

"I do believe we shall suit . . ." Lady Louisa continued, "yes, I think Dr. Ross is quite right, for I am quite looking forward to seeing you fashionably attired."

"But, Lady Louisa," Felicia protested. "I do not think you understand my position. I have no money to buy new clothes."

"Nonsense, my child. You misunderstand me. My son tells me that he neglected to pick up your trunk from the stagecoach and has insisted that he be allowed to refurbish your wardrobe."

Felicia felt herself blush again. She bit her lower lip in consternation. "I cannot possibly accept such a gift," she said quickly. "It would be unseemly, I am sure."

"Quite so, my dear. Quite so. That is just what I told Ian. No, it will be my pleasure to put matters right, and Dr. Ross agrees absolutely. Therapy, he called it. I have asked Ian to send my dressmaker to me as soon as he returns to London. In fact, he decided to post back right away, so she should be here in a couple of days."

Powerless to resist this charming woman, Felicia smiled at her enthusiasm. "Well, maybe one or two would be all right, for on quick reflection I think Mrs. Barton would think very poorly of me if I arrived with only one dress to my name. But I would be much happier if we could keep an accounting of what is spent so that I may repay you when I have received my first quarter's wage."

"We shall see," Lady Louisa responded temperately. "We shall see."

Felicia had to be content with that answer, for Lady Louisa had closed her eyes, making it quite obvious that she had finished with that particular topic.

A comfortable silence fell between them, and Felicia took the opportunity to look about her. The room was not large, but with its southern exposure, was extremely light and airy. The furnishings were of the finest quality and, as Felicia's gaze moved from the intricate, inlaid Regency desk with silver feet tucked away in one corner, she started slightly as she saw the piano, almost hidden behind some plants, in another corner. A chord in her memory was responding to something, but she couldn't place it.

"Go over and see if you can play something," Lady Louisa said quietly. There was a depth of understanding in her voice.

Gracefully, Felicia made her way to the corner and touched the piano gently before she sat down. Putting both hands on the keys she closed her eyes and began playing. The tune that came to her was a simple ballad, and she was able to play it through without a mistake.

"Again, please," Lady Louisa begged. "Only take it a little more slowly, and I will accompany you."

Felicia nodded, a feeling of excitement deep within her. Could this mean that her memory was not lost forever, she wondered. A sense of hope communicated itself to her fingers, and the stiffness vanished from her playing. Exhilarated, she joined Lady Louisa in singing. They were both so engrossed they did not hear Dr. Ross enter.

A becoming blush tinged Felicia's cheeks as she ended the ballad, which deepened when Dr. Ross applauded.

"Bravo! Bravo!" he complimented. "It would seem that we have discovered a lady with hidden talents." He addressed this remark to Lady Louisa who nodded in agreement.

"I do believe that with some practice she would be a very good pianist."

"Do you think to sponsor her?" Dr. Ross inquired.

T'would be better than spending the rest of one's life as a governess, Lady Louisa thought to herself.

"Felicia," Dr. Ross asked abruptly. "Do you remember anything at all about playing a piano?"

"Nothing specific, but I think I can remember other passages. Oh! Dr. Ross, is it a good sign?"

"It is difficult to say at the moment," Dr. Ross hedged, not wanting to build up her hopes. "Although it is an encouraging indication that your unconscious mind is responding to outside stimuli."

Lady Louisa smiled in delight. "And to think, she started to play at my suggestion. I am beginning to like this cure you have prescribed. I declare I feel better already."

Dr. Ross glanced over to Felicia. "Play some more," he encouraged. "I want to hear what else you can remember." Turning to Lady Louisa he said quietly, "I knew you would like her. You know, the more I see of her, the more convinced I am that she is of gentle birth. She has so much dignity in her bearing, and such a cultured voice."

"I agree, Paul," Lady Louisa whispered. "I think it a terrible shame that she has to make a living teaching other people's children. I wonder who she is."

"I hope to have the answer to that before she leaves for Manchester."

"I wish she wouldn't insist on going," Lady Louisa sighed. "I am not at all sure it is the best move for her. Whatever is a beauty like that going to do in such a ghastly town? It is positively unthinkable. Perhaps I should write to my dear friend, Lady Worthing. She has recently taken up residence near Manchester. It is just possible that I can persuade her to check up on this Mrs. Barton. It would simply never do if there were a young Mr. Barton."

Dr. Ross smiled at her ramblings. "You have a point there," he said. "Her striking looks would sweep any callow youth off his feet."

"I will do it!" Lady Louisa said determinedly. "Write to Lady Worthing," she explained as Dr. Ross raised his eyebrows in question. "Pray help me to my desk, Paul, and I will do it this instant."

Felicia left the piano and took Lady Louisa's arm.

"You really do play very well, my dear," Dr. Ross praised. "Very well, indeed. It is easy to hear that you have been well taught."

"Thank you, doctor. I have a feeling that it is something I enjoy as well." She looked down at her fingers and flexed them slightly. "I must be out of practice though, for my fingers are very stiff. I wonder how long it is since I last played."

They had reached the desk by this time, and Lady Louisa settled herself in the bow-legged armchair. Not

wishing Felicia to know of her inquiries, she turned to her
and said, "We don't keep formal hours in the country.
Dinner will be served at six. Paul, pray take Felicia for a
turn in the rose garden. I am sure there are questions you
have to ask her, and I want to finish my correspondence
before the light fades."

They took their leave and left Lady Louisa staring re-
flectively at a blank sheet of paper. Then the steady,
scratching sound of her pen filled the silence and soon the
page was covered with her spidery handwriting. With a
flourish she signed her name and rang the silver bell on
her desk for the butler. Suddenly, she felt it was urgent to
send her missive to Lady Worthing.

The next few days passed very quickly. True to his
word, Lord Umber sent the dressmaker down to Alverston, with private instructions not to mind the cost as he
was footing the bill.

Miss Sophy, as she called herself, was delighted to be
able to dress Felicia. She seldom had the chance to fit her
creations to such a perfect figure. Felicia's waist, without
the aid of a corset, was a mere eighteen inches, and her
bosom was high and firm.

"Magnificent," she murmured to herself as she took the
measurements. "Perfection!"

Mindful of Lord Umber's instructions, she did not
mention the price of any of the materials she had brought
with her. And when Felicia expressed interest in the most
expensive silk, Miss Sophy was quick to allay her fears
about cost.

"Within the budget that be," she soothed. "And just

the right color for you. I can see you now, taking a stroll in that. What a picture you will present."

"Do you think it will be all right?" Felicia asked of Lady Louisa. "I cannot imagine that Mrs. Barton will think such finery is appropriate for a governess."

"But there will be times when you will need a pretty dress," Lady Louisa interposed quickly, hoping that Miss Sophy would forget what she had just heard. She was not anxious to have the word around that Felicia was a servant, and a temporary one at that. No, she cherished the hope that somehow she could persuade Felicia to stay with her permanently.

Miss Sophy smiled to herself. It was always a pleasure doing business with Lord Umber. He was always such a gentleman when it came to paying the bills and never questioned them at all. If this Miss Felicia wanted to pretend she was a governess, that was her business. Miss Sophy was far too discreet to make any comment.

After a day spent choosing patterns and fabrics, Miss Sophy left for London, promising to return within the week with the new wardrobe. Between them, Lady Louisa and Miss Sophy had persuaded Felicia to take five gowns and, unknown to Felicia, Lady Louisa had asked Miss Sophy to make up two evening gowns as well.

Meanwhile, Felicia participated in daily sessions with Dr. Ross. They were not totally unproductive, for while she was in the trance she was able to answer some of the questions about her childhood. However, if Dr. Ross asked her anything about her immediate past, she remembered nothing.

When she was out of the trance, they discussed what

had been learned. After four days they had managed to build a composite picture of her early childhood, which Dr. Ross concluded had been quite normal and happy.

"It really is an interesting case," he said to Lady Louisa over tea one afternoon. "Felicia is well-bred, well-educated, and well-adjusted. Yet I begin to see that something terrible happened to her in the recent past that is the real cause of her amnesia. The blow to her head was not the true cause of her loss of memory."

"Whatever could have happened, do you suppose?" Lady Louisa asked, a worried frown creasing her brow.

"Any number of things. At this stage, all I know is that the true cause is painful. So painful her unconscious mind is refusing to recall it. You haven't heard from your friend in Manchester, I suppose?"

"No, and neither has Felicia heard from her Mrs. Barton. And I am hoping that she never does, for I swear that I have become so fond of her, I cannot bear to think of her ever going away."

"A pity really, for I was hoping Mrs. Barton would provide a key to open more memories," he leaned forward conspiratorily. " 'Tis possible we can between us persuade her to stay, for I am certain that the longer she is here, the less she likes the idea of going to Manchester."

"I am just afraid that it is a little dull for her at Alverston. Mayhap I should ask Ian to come down soon with a house party. If Felicia could mingle with people her own age, do you think that will help?"

Dr. Ross hesitated for a moment. He was pleased that Lady Louisa was showing interest in someone other than herself. It marked a big change in her normally reclusive attitude. But his real concern was for Felicia and how she would react in Lord Umber's presence. Nonetheless, he liked the suggestion. "Medically speaking," he finally replied, "I think it would do you both some good."

Four

When Felicia was informed of the forth-
coming visit, she said nothing, keeping her fears to herself. Dr. Ross sensed her uneasiness but decided not to interfere.

However, her fears diminished as she was caught up in
the whirl of activity that ensued. Extra servants were
hired from the village, and they descended like a swarm
of bees on the house. All the rooms that had been closed
for years were opened and aired. The holland covers were
removed, and the maids were everywhere with their mops
and brooms.

Lady Louisa's misgivings about her ability to cope with
many guests grew as the day for them to arrive drew
nearer. Felicia, who felt a genuine fondness for her, had
to calm her several times.

"I don't think you should worry about the flower arrangements. I will take care of them if you wish. I noticed that James has some beautiful blossoms in the hothouse."

"Would you, Felicia?" Lady Louisa breathed thankfully. "That would relieve me of a big worry. I was never terribly good with flowers. And, I swear I don't know how I am going to cope with all these people that Ian will be bringing down. Why, oh, why did I let Paul talk me into this."

"If the truth were known, Lady Louisa," Felicia said with a smile, "I do believe you are enjoying yourself, in spite of your protestations. And the difference all these preparations have made in the house is miraculous."

"This is how it used to be when Ian's father was alive," Lady Louisa said wistfully. "You are right, Felicia, I am enjoying myself more than I ever dreamed possible. But, however are we going to entertain them all? I am quite out of the habit, you know."

"I am sure Lord Umber will make all the necessary arrangements," Felicia assured her. "If the weather holds, they can go for a picnic, and there are some beautiful trails for rides." A pensive note crept into her voice as she thought of the fun the party would have. "And in the evening, Lord Umber is sure to think up some amusements."

"You are right, of course, dear child. Ian will take care of everything. And you are to join in as well. I will not have you languishing at my side when there are young people around."

"But I cannot possibly," Felicia said crisply. "It is not my place."

"Nonsense! Both Dr. Ross and I feel you will benefit

from spending time in young company. So I will brook no argument."

Before Felicia could protest further, Miss Sophy was announced, and Felicia forgot her apprehension at Lady Louisa's suggestion as she tried on her new dresses.

"If only you could be seen in London," Miss Sophy gushed, much to Felicia's amusement. "What a credit you would be to me. Think of all the business I would get!"

"I am sorry that Manchester is so far away," Felicia laughed. "But maybe I can help you anyway, for Lord Umber is bringing a house party down next weekend, and you may be certain that if anyone asks about my gowns, I will refer them to you." Privately she thought this unlikely, for she had heard all about the sophisticated company Lord Umber kept when away from his mother. It was most improbable that they would ask her advice.

The day of Lord Umber's homecoming finally arrived. When Felicia awoke, she was dismayed to see it was raining. She dressed quickly in her old gown, and ran downstairs to check on the last-minute preparations. Mrs. Keyes, the housekeeper, appeared and had a few questions, which Felicia dealt with before she descended to the kitchens to check on the menu for the first meal. Alphonse, the chef that Lord Umber had sent down from London, was firmly installed in his domain and was not pleased to see Felicia.

"*Mon dieu,* mam'selle Felicia!" he exclaimed in his broken English, "I beg of you to return again. I am too busy now . . . later, perhaps. . . . But I 'ave to prepare zee sauce *spécial* for m'lord."

Felicia smiled at him. "*Non, je n'ai pas besoin de votre*

assistance," she said in perfect French. "I was only checking to see whether *I* could help *you."* She promptly withdrew, and it was only when she reached the main hall that she realized she had actually spoken another language. Knowing that Dr. Ross would be in the library at this time of the morning, she knocked briefly on the door, but in her excitement entered right away. She could not wait another second to tell him her news.

"Dr. Ross," she said in a breathless voice, "I have just discovered that I speak French." Thinking she saw him in the wingback chair near the fireplace, she ran over to him.

"That, my dear Miss Richards, was something I never doubted from the beginning," the disturbing voice of Lord Umber drawled.

"You!" Felicia exclaimed. "Whatever are you doing here?" In her dismay, her tone was sharp.

"I live here," he replied slowly, an amused look in his eyes.

"Where is Dr. Ross?" Felicia demanded. Her heart was pounding and her knees seemed about to give way. She took a deep breath to steady herself. "I am sorry to have intruded, but Dr. Ross is usually here at this time, and anyway," she continued as her spirit returned, "we are not expecting you until this afternoon."

"I am sorry to overset your arrangements then, Miss Richards," he teased. "I decided to ride down early. Perhaps I should have informed you of my change in plans?"

"No, not at all," Felicia replied. "It was just that you took me by surprise."

"Not for the first time, my dear," Lord Umber laughed. "I apologize."

"Oh! . . . you . . . you despicable trifler. How can you call yourself a gentleman, and then recall that incident. I knew it was a mistake to stay here." She moved to the door hastily, but her exit was halted by Lord Umber's voice.

"Now, wait a minute," he said, his voice no longer teasing. "I apologized for that. I admit I made a mistake, which I regret. But if you think that I am going to let you leave my mother when your presence has brought about such a miraculous change in her, you are mistaken."

"You cannot hold me here against my will," Felicia snapped. "And your mother knows that I intend to leave as soon as I have word from Mrs. Barton. So to leave a few days earlier will not matter."

"Mrs. Barton? Who is she?"

"The lady in Manchester," Felicia said in exasperation.

"Oh! Yes. I had forgotten. But you promised to remain until you heard from her, is that right?"

"It is what I promised Dr. Ross, yes. But now, I think it best if I leave immediately."

"Pray do not let my presence cut short your stay," Lord Umber replied, his sense of humor overcoming his annoyance at Felicia's hostility. "If I give you my word, as a gentleman, to behave with utmost propriety, will you agree to do as you originally planned?" His tone was compelling and friendly.

Felicia hesitated and before she could answer, the door was flung open, grazing her shoulder slightly.

"Ian, are you coming?" the voice of a young man called impatiently. "I have been waiting an age for you."

"Pray come in a moment, David, and meet my mother's companion."

Felicia looked down at her drab dress in dismay. Whatever would Lord Umber's friend think of such a dowd.

"Miss Richards," Lord Umber said languidly, "allow me to present a good friend, Mr. Burton. Mr. David Burton."

"Beg pardon, ma'am, didn't mean to startle you," Mr. Burton said as he stepped into the library. "Pleased to meet you." His eyes took in her attire and he wondered silently what such a drab thing was doing as Lady Louisa's companion. Then, he looked at her face, and realized how very beautiful she was.

"How do you do, Mr. Burton," Felicia was saying, her voice unsteady as she stared at his pleasant, open countenance. He shifted his stance uneasily at such close scrutiny, by a young woman.

"I say, Miss Richard," he said at last, "is something the matter? I didn't hurt you, did I?"

Felicia shook her head. "Pray forgive my manners, Mr. Burton. And, no, you didn't hurt me." She brushed her shoulder absent-mindedly. "I thought, for a moment, that I had met you before and I was trying to place the connection." She shook her head, as though trying to clear it.

"Never seen you before," Mr. Burton said hurriedly. "Hardly likely to forget such a face, what, Ian?"

"No, David," Lord Umber agreed lightly, aware that his friend was wondering whether he had indeed met Felicia in some house of ill repute. "But it is interesting to hear Miss Richards say your face is familiar, because this is the young lady I was telling you about. The one who has lost her memory."

A look of relief spread across Mr. Burton's face. "Ah!

Yes. Well, I am sorry, Miss Richards. I wish I could help you, but as far as I know, I have never met you before."

A puzzled look still clouded her eyes as she took her leave. "Perhaps it was a long time ago," she said thoughtfully, the disappointment obvious in her voice. "I am sorry I cannot remember more."

It had stopped raining when Felicia finally found Dr. Ross in the rose garden. She excitedly told him all that had happened. A pleased expression lit up his face as he listened. "We must probe this area further in our next session. It may be only a false trail, but it is worth exploring."

"Who is this Mr. Burton, anyway?" Felicia asked. "It is uncanny how familiar he seems to be."

"A friend of Lord Umber's. A barrister of some repute. The youngest man ever to be admitted to the bar. Very well regarded by his peers."

Felicia looked unimpressed. "But that doesn't help me," she cried, stamping her foot. "Oh, why, why do I think I know him?"

"He could have been the bearer of news at some point in the past." Dr. Ross took her arm reassuringly as he continued gravely. "You must face the fact, Felicia, that you may well be an orphan. Quite frankly, that is the only solution I can think of to explain why you are having to earn your own living. There is no doubt in my mind that you are well born. It could be that Mr. Burton, in his capacity of barrister, had to break the news of your parents' death. So possibly he spoke to a relative of yours—a brother perhaps, if you have one—and you may have caught a glimpse of him. I am sure if he had met with you directly, he would have remembered. I wish I could be more specific, but at the moment I can only conjecture."

"I understand, Dr. Ross, really I do," Felicia said, smiling. "I think I have prepared myself for the worst—about not having a family, I mean."

They paused by the sundial and Felicia gasped as she saw the time. "Thank goodness the sun has come out to remind me of the hour. I must hurry back and change, for the guests will be arriving shortly."

Dr. Ross let go of her arm. "Off with you, then, and don't be so busy that you forget to enjoy yourself."

"No, doctor," she answered with an air of exaggerated decorum. "I will obey your instructions implicitly."

He was on his way to the stables thinking to find his host there when the butler approached him. "If you are not too busy, Dr. Ross, Lord Umber would like a word with you. He is in the library."

"The very thing," Dr. Ross muttered to himself, as he followed the retreating figure of the servant.

Dr. Ross was surprised to find Lady Louisa ensconced on the sofa in the library, with Lord Umber standing at the window. "Good afternoon, ma'am, Ian. You wanted to see me?"

Lord Umber walked forward with his hand outstretched. "Paul, good to see you. A drink?" He indicated a tray filled with gleaming crystal.

"Not yet awhile, Ian. Think I will save myself for the festivities tonight. I hear Alphonse has been let loose in the kitchens."

"Sorry to drag you away from the roses, Paul," Lord Umber said, "but I wanted to hear your prognosis on

Miss Richards. My mother tells me that the bits and pieces she has remembered have not been too helpful."

"In essence that is correct, Ian. However, I am beginning to make some headway. I need time though, especially now when she thinks she knows David. This is the first real breakthrough I have had in the case. Maybe another piece of the puzzle will fall into place when we hear from Manchester. No word yet, I suppose, Lady Louisa?"

"No, thank goodness," Lady Louisa replied quickly. "And frankly, I don't wish ever to hear."

Dr. Ross shook his head in a sympathetic gesture. "My real problem is time," he continued, turning to Lord Umber. "I have just received word from my associate that I am needed in London." He fingered the letter he had received that morning that still lay in a pocket. "And frankly, I have no alternative but to take my leave on Sunday."

"But what will happen to Felicia?" Lady Louisa cried. "Oh, dear, is there nothing we can do?"

Lord Umber glanced at Dr. Ross with raised eyebrows. "As a doctor you have a remedy, I am sure. What do you propose?"

"It really depends on Lady Louisa. If she will agree to the scheme I suggest, I think everyone will benefit."

Both men turned to Lady Louisa, who was now sitting up alertly. "Pray continue, Paul," she ordered. "You have me in a positive lather of curiosity."

His reply, after a moment's hesitation, was blunt. "Go to London on an extended visit."

A stunned silence followed. All three were aware that

Lady Louisa has refused to leave Alverston since her husband's death six years ago.

"I cannot possibly," Lady Louisa protested. "I mean, how can I?" She paused as she gave the idea some thought. "Do you really think I am well enough to travel, Paul?" she asked incredulously.

Lord Umber gave a bark of laughter. "I hardly think Paul would make such an outrageous suggestion, Mama, if he thought otherwise. Paul?"

"If you can both bear the cliché, it's just what the doctor is ordering. To be quite honest with you, Lady Louisa, you have no real need of my services any longer. Physically you are in perfect health, and if you can cope with the *idea* of a long journey, the mental rewards you will gain from a London Season will complete the cure."

"I think the suggestion is marvelous, Paul," Lord Umber intervened hastily, as he saw his mother about to protest. "Can we leave it to you to inform Miss Richards?" His voice was light, but Dr. Ross saw the doubt in his eyes.

He had always been amazed by the depth of Lord Umber's affection for his mother. If one were to judge him by outward appearances, one would have called him a cynical libertine. He was well known in every gambling hall in London and the gossip about town gave him the reputation of being a dissolute rakehell. Very few people knew the real man, for Lord Umber went to great lengths to conceal his true character. Apart from insuring that his mother lived in utmost comfort, he quietly worked for several charities, donating and raising large sums of money for orphans. There was an unknown quality about him that set him apart from other men, and his few close friends knew him to be a sensitive, compelling person whom they admired and respected. They knew that, despite his reputation as a roué and his genuine enjoyment of female companionship, he was as often the pursued as the pursuer. Moreover, his personal sense of honor forbade him to seduce any woman who did not come to him freely, and, far from delighting in heartlessly discarding the wantons with whom he tarried (or in severing with unnecessary harshness the alliances instigated by highborn flirts), he took pride in arranging any inevitable farewells with great consideration.

Dr. Ross could well guess what had transpired between Felicia and Lord Umber the day of the accident and understood how Lord Umber felt when he realized the mistake he had made—angry with himself and now dismayed at the prospect that Felicia might refuse to go to London on account of his behavior.

"I think I can persuade her, although I am sure she will worry about the difference in the stagecoach fare from London to Manchester."

"Assure her that I will compensate her," Lady Louisa said. "As I am powerless to resist you both, I will need her to travel with me. The very thought of embarking on such a journey by myself is frightening."

"Of course, Lady Louisa," Dr. Ross smiled triumphantly.

"I know we can rely on you, Paul," Lord Umber said, turning to his mother, "I will escort both you and Miss Richards to London in a week—if that is convenient, Mama?"

"Convenient!" Lady Louisa exclaimed in mock horror.

"Since when have you been concerned with anyone else's convenience?"

"Seldom, Mama," Lord Umber replied, repressing a smile. "This is one of those very rare occasions."

"And what of our house guests?" Lady Louisa inquired.

"Oh! Not to worry on their account," Lord Umber assured. "For I am sure that after a few days of idleness they will all be happy to return to London."

Acknowledging that all was settled with a nod of her silvery head, Lady Louisa rose from the sofa. "Well, in that case, gentlemen, I can see that I will barely have time to rest in the next week unless I start making the necessary arrangements now. Paul, if I did not know better, I would swear you are in league with my son."

She left the room without a backward glance and did not see the two men smile at each other in amusement.

"Well, Ian," Dr. Ross asked, "do you approve of the change in your mother?"

"You have worked a miracle, Paul. I never thought I would ever see her sparkle like that again. It has been such a long time."

"Your thanks should go to Miss Richards, for 'tis she who was wrought the change."

"Aha! Miss Richards!" Lord Umber said nonchalantly. "If I did not know you better, Paul, I would suggest you have fixed your interest in that direction."

"Only professionally," Dr. Ross responded quickly. "Although 'twould be difficult to find such a sweet-natured female again. She is a real puzzlement to me, Ian. I declare she is as well-bred as either you or I, and yet, I have never heard of a Richards in our circles."

"It could be that she is using a false name," Lord Umber suggested. "Who knows, someone may recognize her in London and solve the mystery for you."

"But not for her," Dr. Ross pointed out. "It has become imperative to me that I restore her memory for her. Can you imagine the horror of not knowing who you really are?"

"Consider the possibility, Paul, that she may be better off not knowing. Suppose she really is a highly accomplished cyprian. That could explain her knowledge and manners."

Dr. Ross pretended to look shocked. "Ian, my dear friend, you are far too young to be such a cynic. Mark my words, Miss Richards is what she seems to be. A lady of quality."

"Enough, Paul," Lord Umber laughed. "I hear the sounds of my guests arriving."

"Your latest flirt amongst them?" Dr. Ross questioned lightly.

"The delicious Lady Barbara? Oh, yes. But I very much doubt that she will arrive early. She will be late enough to make a grand entrance, but not so late as to appear rude. Excuse me, Paul," he gave a slight bow. "Duty calls."

Five

     Felicia paused at the bottom of the formal staircase to admire the floral display she had arranged. A maid had placed it on the large, hand-carved oak pedestal that one of Lord Umber's ancestors had brought back from the West Indies. The fragrance from the flowers filled the hallway. Lilies of the valley interwoven with delphiniums set off to perfection the delicate, almost translucent white orchids she had discovered in one of the greenhouses. Seeing her handiwork, she felt pleased. Even if she could not remember under what circumstances, for the moment, it was reassuring to know that she had been raised to take care of domestic details.

"I think they will please his lordship," she said to herself as she crossed the tiled floor to the green drawing room. "And I am certain that Lady Louisa will enjoy them."

She slipped into the room unobtrusively and found, to her dismay, that a few of the guests were already assembled. She quickly made her way to Lady Louisa's side, but her desire to go unnoticed was thwarted when David Burton detached himself from a group of people and joined her.

"Good evening, Lady Louisa, Miss Richards," he said as he bowed deeply. "What a charming picture you both make. You quite brighten up this dark corner."

Felicia blushed prettily and Lady Louisa chuckled. "Go and make an elegant leg to Miss Fitzroy, David, and take Miss Richards with you. I refuse to be cast into the shade by having her stand next to me."

Mr. Burton smiled. "That will be my pleasure, Lady Louisa," he answered and drew Felicia's hand onto his arm. "Miss Richards?"

Felicia curtsied and moved gracefully toward the group in the center of the room, unaware that everyone was looking at her for she was busy whispering to Mr. Burton, "It is not necessary to introduce me around. After all, I am Lady Louisa's companion, not a relative."

"What? And be accused by all my friends of keeping you all to myself? They would never forgive me." He drew her deftly into the group and made the introductions quickly. He knew they would all be curious as to who she was, but also knew that their good manners would prevail and keep their questions for later.

He had barely recognized in Felicia the dowdy girl he had met earlier in the library. The dress she wore now was the height of fashion, and fitted beautifully. It was light blue silk falling to the ground in soft pleats, and was caught at the waist by a girdle of roses. A frill of sapphire chiffon framed her alabaster white shoulders. Matching roses were threaded through the curls that Lady Louisa's maid had coaxed into a Psyche knot, with a few careless tendrils caressing her cheeks.

She acknowledged the introductions with a polite nod and stood to one side, listening to the general talk, trying to remember all the names.

Lord Rowbotham, a dandy of the first water, eyed her appreciatively. He liked what he saw and wondered if she also had a fortune. He regretfully decided that the answer must be negative, for Lord Umber would have mentioned it. He beamed at her anyway and sidled over to her.

Felicia tried to suppress a smile at the sight he made, and almost succeeded until she caught Mr. Burton's eye. However, she managed to turn her smile into one of polite inquiry which set Lord Rowbotham at ease.

"I say, Miss Richards, what's the latest *on dit* about Umber and his orchids?"

Taken aback by the question, Felicia stared at him blankly. "I beg your pardon? Orchids? I am afraid I don't understand."

"Flowers, you know," he explained kindly. "I noticed a maid putting a whole display of them in the hallway on my way down tonight. Never thought that Umber would agree to wasting those precious blooms on us."

"He didn't," Felicia replied faintly, as a cold feeling gripped her. "I cut them myself."

Lord Rowbotham looked at her in amazement. "You mean he ain't even seen them yet? I thought it peculiar when I saw them. They are far better than mine, and he would easily have won the contest . . ."

"You mean that he was growing them especially for an

exhibition?" Felicia queried. She wondered why Lady Louisa had not said anything, and then remembered that she had cut them at the last moment, without consulting her.

"Far worse," Lord Rowbotham said gravely. "A wager."

"I fear he will not be pleased then." At the moment she felt only disdain for her host. Gambling was such a petty reason to grow such magnificent blooms.

Lord Rowbotham nodded his head in agreement before saying placatingly, "But he cannot blame you, if you didn't know what they were, now can he? What say you, David?"

Mr. Burton raised a questioning eyebrow. "What's that, Cuthbert?"

"The orchids that Miss Richards has cut by mistake. Ian will understand?"

"No, as you well know yourself, Cuthbert." Mr. Burton gave Felicia a sympathetic look. "But do not worry, Miss Richards. I will defend you if Lord Umber allows his temper to get out of control. And, I daresay we can persuade Cuthbert to stand firm on your other side."

"Not wise, David, old boy!" Lord Rowbotham said evasively. "He'll only think I had a hand in it."

Felicia turned to Mr. Burton in disbelief. "You are serious? I can hardly believe that I have committed an unpardonable sin."

Mr. Burton looked at her curiously as he nodded his head. He was surprised that she showed no signs of trepidation.

"Then I shall confess immediately and take all the

heat," she continued determinedly. "Lord Umber will understand, I am sure."

"Yes, yes," Lord Rowbotham agreed quickly. "Ian can never resist a pretty face."

"Shame on you, Cuthbert," Mr. Burton chided. "I, for one, do not intend to let Miss Richards bear the brunt of Ian's fury." He turned toward the rest of the group, who were all listening with interest.

"Oh, Miss Richards," Miss Fitzroy breathed, a look of awe on her plain face. "You are brave."

"Nonsense," Felicia replied, checking the irritation she felt at the way her one simple action had now become the focal point of conversation. "Excuse me, I will go and apologize to Lord Umber immediately, and clear his mind of the thought that you might have had something to do with it, Lord Rowbotham." She dropped a brief curtsy and turned towards the door.

"I will escort you," Mr. Burton said, as he followed her. "There is no need for you to put your head in the lion's mouth without someone standing by to make sure there is fair play."

The determined look left her face as she laughed, "I fear Lord Rowbotham has exaggerated the peril ahead. Surely no one can be that put out by a few cut orchids. It is not as though I took them all."

Mr. Burton shook his head in mock gravity. "It is not so much the orchids, Miss Richards, even though he views them in much the same light as a servant would view a few gold guineas. No, it is more that he does not like to lose a wager. But, come, let us break the news to him and take our punishment bravely."

As the door closed behind them, Miss Fitzroy said to

no one in particular, "Whoever is she? I have never heard of a Miss Richards."

"Some distant relation," Lord Rowbotham said grandly puffing out his chest importantly. It was not often that he was able to hold anyone's attention for long, because normally he talked only about flowers. And very few of his acquaintances knew a sepal from a petal.

"Where did you get that, Cuthbert?" a Mr. Gibbons twitted. "The wisteria around the front door?"

Lord Rowbotham looked down his long nose haughtily. He was well aware that people regarded him as slightly eccentric, for the word had long since leaked out that he talked to his plants. "As a matter of fact, Lord Umber told me himself this afternoon. Didn't mention anything about a fortune, though," he finished morosely.

Mr. Gibbons smirked in unkindly fashion. Everyone knew that Cuthbert had to marry money. "So even though she be ripe for the picking, you have no interest. Tut! Tut! Cuthbert!"

"Oh!" signed Miss Fitzroy in relief. "I'll be sure to tell Barbara . . . I would not like her to be uneasy. . . ." She stopped as she realized no one was listening. Everybody's attention had been caught by the grand entrance of Lady Barbara. She looked stunning in a low-cut dress of orange silk, and her auburn-streaked hair, piled high, set off her finely chiseled features to perfection. The only thing to mar her looks was a small frown of annoyance that creased her brow. This was caused by the absence of Lord Umber. Her eyes scanned the room quickly, but her search failed to recognize him among those already assembled. She tapped her foot in frustration, for she had been certain that he had descended a full five minutes before her, and that surely should have been sufficient time for him to be here to greet her. When she had arrived earlier in the afternoon, he had not seen fit to welcome her, and it was outside of enough that her traveling companion, cousin Milly Fitzroy, witnessed that failing. But for it to happen again—and with Milly grinning at her sympathetically. Why, it . . . it was . . . Oh, she should have heeded her mother's advice and refused the invitation to come to Alverston.

Her attention was finally caught by Lady Louisa, and hastily putting on a smile, she picked her way daintily across the room.

"My dear Barbara," Lady Louisa gushed, her smile equally as dissembling as her guest's. "How are you? And how is your dear mother? Come, be seated, and let us have a cose." She patted an uncomfortable, upright chair near her, and Lady Barbara reluctantly complied with the request.

"Mama is as well as can be expected, thank you. And I am to be sure to pass on all good wishes to you, Lady Louisa." She said the words automatically, but her attention was elsewhere. Seated as she was, with her back to the door, it was impossible for her to see when Lord Umber entered. And how could she show herself to the best advantage if she was at such a disadvantage?

Lady Louisa hid a small smile of satisfaction as she guessed what was in Barbara's mind. She had been unhappy ever since she had heard the rumors of her son's pursuit of Barbara and now, having met her, she was not at all pleased. There was something about Barbara that she could not like. An air of superiority, perhaps, or the way Barbara seemed to delight in focusing attention on herself. She displayed such forwardness for one so young. Lady Louisa shrugged.

Unfortunately, at that precise moment, her son was displaying no sense at all. Mr. Burton had been quite correct in his prediction of the irrational way his friend would react to the news, and with an anger that surprised even himself Lord Umber berated Felicia.

"By whose leave do you have the right to make yourself so completely at home that you have the temerity to pick my orchids?" he demanded. "I cannot think how I let myself be persuaded that you would make a suitable companion for my mother."

"I say, Ian," Mr. Burton interjected, "that's doing it a bit brown, isn't it?"

"Never mind, Mr. Burton," Felicia said icily. "Lord Umber has already made it quite clear the position he thinks I would suit." To his own annoyance Lord Umber flushed at this reminder of the original misunderstanding between them. She continued, "However, if I have proven myself so unsatisfactory, I shall leave for Manchester on the morrow. I am more than sorry that I dared interfere with your orchids, m'lord, but I can hardly make amends now. I can only assure you that there are several perfectly healthy blooms that will surely win you your wager." Both men started at the disdain in her voice. With an air of unconcern, Felicia turned to Mr. Burton. "If you will kindly escort me back to the salon, I will bid my farewells to Lady Louisa and endeavor to ready myself to leave here by first light."

Lord Umber frowned at her. *Damn the girl and her composure,* he thought, then wished he had not been so hasty with his words. But how could he have known that she would react with such forceful determination. He had spoken unthinkingly, out of frustration. "That will not be necessary, Miss Richards," he said hastily as he realized that they were nearing the door. "I accept your apologies and assurances that you will do nothing untoward for the remainder of your stay here."

Felicia was about to make an angry retort, when Mr. Burton broke in hastily. "Come, now. I cannot believe that either of you are in earnest. Let us not mar the evening ahead by a fit of pique, else the rest of the guests will surely find some excuse to return to town in the morning."

"Ever the diplomat, eh, David?" Lord Umber murmured. He glanced at Felicia and noticed that her rigid stance relaxed slightly under Mr. Burton's kindly gaze. A feeling of annoyance surged through him. This was the first time he had ever noticed David's defending a lady, and it bothered him. He shrugged his shoulders slightly. "Shall we join the others?" he asked casually and led the way to the green salon.

Lady Louisa was looking anxiously toward the door when the three entered. She frowned at the expression on her son's face and wondered what could have upset him. However, the scowl lifted when he saw his mother and his ill humor dissipated as he looked with appreciation at the entrancing figure of Lady Barbara. He strolled over to his latest flirt, making an elegant leg while apologizing profusely for his tardiness. Within seconds he had her laughing, and Lady Louisa was left to ponder whether Felicia . had been the witting or unwitting cause of her son's black mood.

Six

Felicia's emotions were in a turmoil all evening and she was thankful when dinner was over and she could retire. Lady Louisa reluctantly accepted her excuse of a headache, but saw that Felicia was unhappy about something.

Now, in the daylight, with the sun shining through her bedroom curtains, Felicia wondered if last night had not been a nightmare. But no, for she would never forget the dark looks Lord Umber had thrown at her throughout the meal. How they had contrasted with the seemingly genuine smiles of affection he bestowed on Lady Barbara. And she was still smarting from the sharp words he had used after her light-hearted confession. It was only Mr. Burton's intervention that had prevented their exchanging further hard words, words that Felicia knew she certainly would have regretted later. For whatever her feelings toward Lord Umber, she had grown exceedingly fond of Lady Louisa and did not want to cause her benefactress any undue stress.

Only yesterday, Lady Louisa had confided in Felicia her fears about her son. His reputation was irksome to her, but the gossip about his latest flirt filled her with dread that he might be seriously considering marriage. At this point, she had not met Lady Barbara, but her overactive imagination had conjured up horrendous images of Barbara and she liked none of them. These were caused, in the main, by her acquaintance with Barbara's mother, whom Lady Louisa had known since childhood. "A more grasping, haughty, argumentative woman I have yet to meet." And the word had reached her at Alverston that Barbara took after her mother.

Felicia shook off her feeling of depression and went downstairs in search of Dr. Ross. She wanted to see him one last time before he set off for London. She made for the rose garden and, as she passed the conservatory that housed the remaining orchids, she pulled a wry face.

"That hardly encourages the growth of such sensitive blooms, Miss Richards," a voice murmured behind her.

She whirled around and was appalled to see Lord Umber smiling down at her sardonically.

"I am told I must apologize for my behavior last night," he continued, ignoring her exclamation of dismay. "Your champion, Mr. Burton, is quite out of patience with me."

"Indeed, sir," Felicia sputtered, her eyes glinting dangerously. "Your apologies are not necessary. I do confess that I found your reaction to my simple mistake puzzling. . . ."

"Simple mistake!" he exclaimed. "You could have cost me ten thousand guineas."

Felicia gasped at his words, but the contempt she had felt earlier at the talk of gambling welled up within her. His words proved he too was a hardened gambler. " 'Tis less than the price of a house in Richmond," she said calmly and then instantly regretted her words as she saw the look of disgust spread over Lord Umber's face. Bracing herself for another verbal attack, she drew herself up and squared her shoulders defensively.

This simple action completely disarmed Lord Umber, and the torrent of words he was about to hurl at her died on his lips. He realized, suddenly, how vulnerable she was. His annoyance over the misappropriation of his orchids had long since evaporated, and when David had reapproached him for his appalling lack of manners, he had felt somewhat remorseful. How he wished he had not stumbled across that overturned coach.

He glanced at Felicia and felt himself smiling at her. What a provoking chit she was, to be sure. He slowly took her hand and raised it to his lips. Brushing the back of it lightly, he said softly, "Forgive me, Miss Richards. I had not meant to cause you any unhappiness."

Felicia snatched her hand away, surprised by the unexpected tenderness in his voice and aware only of the tingling sensation his kiss had left—the same feeling she had experienced the first time he had kissed her. "No . . . no," she managed. "It is I who should be reinforcing my apologies. I must learn to think before I speak so rashly."

"And I must try not to be so provoking." His smile

widened and for a moment they looked into each other's eyes. A strange feeling spread through Felicia, and she felt herself returning his smile.

They were still gazing at each other quietly when Dr. Ross walked up to them. He sensed the tension between them and misinterpreting it, quickly drew Felicia away. "If you do not mind, Ian," he said briskly, "I would like a few words with Miss Richards before I take my leave."

"Certainly, Paul," Lord Umber returned quietly, feeling quite shaken by his actions. "I must see to the well-being of my guests anyway." He gave Felicia a cursory bow and turned on his heel sharply. He was thankful for the interruption, for he knew that if he had been alone with Felicia for much longer he would have gathered her into his arms and kissed her again.

He entered the house through the French windows of his study and was surprised to see Lady Barbara standing by his desk. She turned at his footstep and gave a breathless giggle.

"Oh! How you frightened me, Sir Ian!" she trilled. "I was looking for something to sharpen my quill with." She held out a pen helplessly.

"You should have asked one of the servants," Lord Umber replied tartly, as he moved over to her and took the proffered implement. "I do believe there are one or two on duty in the hall." His light smile took the edge off his words and Lady Barbara relaxed. It appeared that her ruse had worked, and a small light of triumph lit her beady eyes.

She had been perturbed by his behavior toward her last night, and she had confided in Cousin Milly before they had retired that she feared his ardor for her was waning.

She had, consequently, been quite determined to force a meeting with him this morning and had purposely risen early in order to snare him before breakfast. Cousin Milly had been horrified, but then Cousin Milly had such antiquated notions.

"They all seemed so busy with breakfast, I did not want to make a nuisance of myself."

Lord Umber looked at her obliquely and hid the disdainful look these words prompted behind the quill. One thing he knew for certain about Barbara, and that was she would never give a second thought whom she bothered if she wanted something done.

"So thoughtful of you, Lady Barbara," he murmured. He bent over, took a knife from the top drawer of his desk, and whittled a new point on the pen. "There, I think that should suffice," he continued. "Although I do not think you will have time to use it today. I have planned a picnic and, if we are to reach our destination before noon, we should set out as soon as breakfast is over."

Lady Barbara clapped her hands in delight. "Oh! What a wonderful plan! I do so love picnics. Do we ride or take our carriages?" Her busy mind was picturing the various outfits she had brought and knew that her new green velvet riding habit would be sensational. So without waiting for a reply, she breathed, "Please say we are to ride."

Lord Umber felt his mood softening slightly. After the confused meeting he had just had with Felicia, Lady Barbara's artless chatter was strangely soothing.

"I would be delighted to ride with you, Lady Barbara. I shall, of course, provide a carriage for those who are interested in maintaining a more leisurely pace. If you will excuse me, I will inform the others of the arrangements."

He was gone before she could reply, and the only witness to the complacent look on her face was the stern portrait of Lord Umber's father.

The picnic was a huge success. The mild weather held, and the few clouds that gathered during the morning posed no real threat to the party. Lord Umber had thoughtfully sent his groom and two servants ahead to the spot he had chosen for luncheon, so by the time all his guests arrived, the food had been spread out on pure white linen clothes on the grass.

Felicia's absence went unnoticed by everyone except David Burton, and when he inquired mildly of Lord Umber where she was, Lord Umber snapped, "I do not know. She made mother the excuse." He had been looking forward to her presence at the picnic, and his disappointment was strong when she had made a feeble excuse about being unable to attend.

Lady Barbara overheard the remark and nodded her head contentedly. His tone certainly indicated that he had no interest in his distant relation, even though Cousin Milly had warned her that there was always a danger with one so serene and pretty as Felicia.

Her mood of contentment lasted until after dinner that evening. Lord Umber had singled her out all day, making it perfectly clear to the entire company that he found her attractive and charming. His caustic comments made her laugh, and her ability to mimic the most pretentious people of their acquaintance obviously amused him. A becoming blush heightened her lovely features as she acknowledged the envious looks Cousin Milly and a few other ladies threw in her direction.

However, when Lady Louisa suggested a musical interlude, it was Felicia who was asked to play the piano. Within minutes of Felicia's playing, it was perfectly clear that she was talented. And, when she finished, the entire company broke into spontaneous applause.

It angered Lady Barbara that she was no longer the center of attention, and she snapped her fan closed impatiently.

"Isn't she marvellous?" Cousin Milly breathed in her ear. "I do not think I have ever heard a better interpretation of Chopin."

"You have never heard me play," Lady Barbara responded sharply, oblivious to the fact that Lord Umber was standing directly behind her.

"Unworthy, Lady Barbara," he murmured good-naturedly, before he moved away.

"But the truth," she retorted unabashed.

"Barbara!" Cousin Milly exclaimed. "How could you? 'Tis most unseemly to express such emotion."

The unexpected rebuke from her cousin caused Lady Barbara to frown, but she acknowledged the truth of the words. "You are right as usual, Milly. I will endeavor to mind my tongue in the future." She glanced across at Lord Umber, who seemed to be deep in conversation with Lord Rowbotham, and the brittle smile faded from her face.

Felicia refused all pleas for an encore, for she was acutely conscious of the fury emanating from Lady Barbara. She wondered if Lord Umber had anything to do with it. As she glanced over to him, she was surprised to see that he was already looking in her direction. She dropped her eyes to the floor in confusion and rose quickly from the piano stool. Suddenly aware of his presence, she wished that she had escaped to the protective side of Lady Louisa earlier. She had managed to avoid him all day, since their confrontation in the rose garden, but now, here he was, bearing down on her with a rakish grin on his handsome face.

"You have been remarkably well taught, Miss Richards," he said softly. "Quite obviously by a master. Indeed, you have us all in awe of your ability."

His compliments confused her further. Had he been his usual irritating self, she would have known how to respond.

"Oh nonsense, Lord Umber," she replied brusquely. "I am sure my playing is no more than adequate. Why, I am certain Lady Barbara is better equipped to give us a real concert."

"You two should deal famously together, then, for she is of the same mind."

Felicia flashed him an angry look, but his eyes mocked her, and she held back her retort.

"I assure you she is," he continued urbanely, "for I heard her say so myself."

He moved away on these words, leaving her smiling reluctantly. He really is a rogue, she thought, but that would explain the hostility she had felt in the atmosphere. Aware that her conversation had been watched by Lady Barbara, she broadened her smile and made her way to the love seat that lady occupied.

"Lord Umber was telling me how exquisitely you play," she said smoothly. "I beg that you do us the honor of entertaining us, for it would give me great pleasure to hear some of the tunes I struggle with played by an expert."

Flattered by such talk, Lady Barbara agreed and made her way to the piano. Felicia settled herself more comfortably on the love seat and thought smugly that Lord Umber had been well served, for now he would have to turn the pages of music for his flirt.

He threw her a glowering look as he complied with Lady Barbara's request, but failed to notice the mischievous gleam in Felicia's eye. She enjoyed the discomfort he was displaying.

He could no longer deny the fact to himself, that after a day spent in Lady Barbara's company her charms were palling and he was beginning to regret the impulse that had caused him to pursue her. She was an empty-headed, vain little puss, who agreed with everything he said. The realization that she bored him came as no real surprise, for it was something that always happened, but what did surprise him was that it happened so quickly. Not that any woman had been able to hold his interest long except for Janie Slagle, but then his relationship with her was entirely different. And now he was beginning to despair that he would ever meet someone whom he could accept as a marriage partner. He knew his mother was worried over his seemingly loose ways, and more than anything he would like to allay her fears. But he simply could not enter a marriage devoid of mutual respect.

He looked down at Lady Barbara and realized that he had not heard a note she had played. He mentally shook himself awake in time to applaud her and then moved away to speak to David Burton.

The next few days passed quickly. He managed to escape any intimate encounters with Lady Barbara but found himself increasingly annoyed by the amused looks he caught Felicia casting in his direction.

Lady Louisa, thankful that her son's pursuit of Lady Barbara was apparently fading, relaxed and began to enjoy herself and the idea of her upcoming journey to London.

"I can be quite comfortable now," she said to Felicia. "For it is obvious that Ian is not going to make an offer in *that* direction."

Felicia agreed with a little laugh, for she was feeling in unusually high spirits. "In sooth, ma'am, I believe you are right. But I fear Lady Barbara had not yet realized it. I declare she is making a proper peagoose of herself. Even Lord Rowbotham noticed that your son's attitude has changed."

Lady Louisa tried to look suitably shocked at the idea that Lord Rowbotham would be so forward as to discuss such delicate matters with a woman, but her disapproving "Tut! Tut!" caused Felicia to giggle again.

"He compared her to the fairest rose, ma'am. 'Perfection,' he said, 'like a rose, has to have constant attention, if it is to be maintained. And already I perceive a crack.' "

They both laughed at this.

"I would never have believed Cuthbert to be so observant," Lady Louisa said and changed the subject hastily as she saw Mr. Burton approaching.

That Felicia was enjoying herself in the company was obvious. Both Lord Rowbotham and Mr. Burton were in constant attendance and even Lord Umber did his best to be civil. Felicia did not mistake the attentions of either gentlemen. Lord Rowbotham was happy to find someone who would listen to his latest theories on raising hybrid roses, and Mr. Burton, it seemed, had set himself up as her protector. She might have been perturbed if she had known that Dr. Ross was responsible for this arrangement but, happy in her ignorance, she basked in the unaccustomed friendly atmosphere. Even the haughty demeanor of Lady Barbara failed to puncture her cheerful mood. The only shadow on her enjoyment was the fact that she was still unable to remember much of her past.

A grudging respect was growing between herself and Lord Umber. Lady Louisa had let slip some details of his charity work and when the opportunity arose, Felicia asked Mr. Burton what these *good works* were all about.

"That is something you must ask Ian, yourself, Miss Richards, for he is quite reticent on the subject. The only information I have is privileged."

Felicia nodded in understanding, but knew she would never have the courage to raise the topic with Lord Umber. The thought that he was more than just a rake was comforting though, and she was able to observe more clearly the small things he did to insure his mother's comfort and the pride he showed in the good management of his estate.

Even Lady Barbara noticed the newfound harmony between the two antagonists and doubled her efforts to be charming whenever Lord Umber was in her vicinity. That she was not going to bring him up to scratch did not enter her mind until Cousin Milly timidly observed that while Lord Umber was always pleasant, he no longer paid her special court.

"Oh, don't be so silly, Milly," Lady Barbara snapped. "He is so busy dancing attendance on his mother, and consulting with his bailiff. He spends as much time as he can with me."

"I . . . I saw him laughing with Miss Richards in the rose garden this morning," Milly stammered. "For a full . . . twenty minutes. . . ." she concluded in an outburst of confidence.

"Pay no heed to that little country mouse, Milly. She had neither the sophistication nor wit to hold the attention of someone so worldly as Lord Umber."

"But she is pretty," Milly persisted. "And Lady Louisa quite dotes on her."

"Enough of your chatter, Cousin, you know so little of such things."

Milly lapsed into a hurt silence as she wondered when Barbara would face the awful reality that Lord Umber did not care enough to propose. Sighing sadly to herself, she picked up her tatting and continued with her work. She really liked Felicia, but felt somewhat guilty about this and was afraid that Barbara would consider her disloyal. How awkward it was all becoming, and how she wished she was back in the safety of her own home.

Her words, however, caused Lady Barbara to observe Felicia and Lord Umber more closely and, by the time her visit was over, she realized that perhaps Milly was right for once. Somehow, Lord Umber had escaped the intricate web she had woven to ensnare him, and now she would have to try other tactics. Either that, or become the laughing stock of London.

Seven

Lady Louisa's arrival halfway through the Season caused a great stir among her friends and acquaintances. For years they had all been trying to persuade her to return to London, and now here she was with the loveliest young lady imaginable in tow. Everyone's curiosity was aroused when they first saw Felicia, and there was much speculation as to who she was.

Both Lord Umber and Lady Louisa were noncommittal. In fact Lord Umber was careful not to appear too frequently in public with his mother, for he was loath to give the impression that he was dangling after Felicia. Not that he should have worried, for the betting at White's was heavily on his announcing his engagement to the Lady Barbara Whitelaw. His pursuit of that auburn-haired beauty had caused no little stir and much jealousy, for she was the belle of the Season and the most sought-after heiress in several years.

Felicia seemed unaware of the questioning looks she received, for she was far too intent on enjoying herself. She had long since overcome her reluctance to accompany Lady Louisa, for as Dr. Ross had explained, "This journey serves two purposes, Miss Richards. First, Lady Louisa will benefit greatly from a change of scene. Secondly, and more importantly for you, someone may recognize you in London and be able to identify you."

"I shall feel like a horse at Tattersall's" she had protested, "with everyone looking for my finer points." She paused as she thought of Lord Umber. His attitude toward her had had a lot to do with her unwillingness to comply with Dr. Ross's request. But now she was not disconcerted by him anymore, in fact, she actually enjoyed his company sometimes. She just wished that they did not argue and misunderstand each other so often.

"I cannot force you, Miss Richards," Dr. Ross had said judiciously. "I want you to take your time to think about what I have suggested, before you say yes or no."

Felicia narrowed her eyes thoughtfully. "I cannot have you thinking me pusillanimous, Dr. Ross," she replied with spirit. "It would also be selfish of me to deprive Lady Louisa of such a peregination. So, yes, I agree to go, providing everyone understands that as soon as word comes from Mrs. Barton, I leave for Manchester."

"That's my girl," he said approvingly. "And your wish about Manchester is understood. Only we will worry about that when the time comes."

The knocker had not been up two days on the house in

Berkeley Square, and already the callers were arriving in a continuous flow.

" 'Tis remarkable," Lady Louisa said, as the ladies were partaking their coffee in the small, blue drawing room on the second evening in town, "how few quiet moments there are. I had quite forgotten how exhausting it can all become. There will be parties we must attend and, of course, I must secure vouchers for Almack's."

Felicia smiled at the excitement in Lady Louisa's voice. It was quite obvious that her popularity had not diminished one whit during her absence.

"I have a card here from Lady Jersey, inviting us to tea the day after tomorrow," Lady Louisa continued. "We shall go, of course, but I do not want you to mention you are my companion."

"Whyever not, ma'am?" Felicia asked in surprise.

"Lady Jersey is your entree to Almack's, dear child. Only she will not lift a finger to help if she knows you are about to become a governess."

"I do not want to deceive anyone," Felicia argued. "It would be most embarrassing if word leaked out and people started gossiping. Why, you would become the laughingstock of London."

Lady Louisa laughed gaily. "Not at all, child. No one will suspect the truth, and I want to make sure you go to Manchester with happy memories. Anyway, Ian has already put the word about that you are a distant relation."

"Really, Lady Louisa," Felicia protested, "I would prefer that you not insist. Besides, I do not want to go to the expense of buying more gowns that will be totally unsuitable when I leave here."

"You are acting like an antiquated old fidget, Felicia,"

Lady Louisa admonished. "I took the liberty of ordering you some ball gowns when Miss Sophy came down to Alverston." She raised a hand to prevent Felicia from protesting further. "And I simply refuse to listen to any objections you may have. It is not good for my health." Her eyes sparkled with laughter as she watched Felicia move uncomfortably in her chair. "There, child. I admire your spirit of independence greatly, but you must learn to bend sometimes, especially to satisfy the whims of an old lady."

An involuntary chuckle escaped Felicia. "You leave me no alternative, ma'am, but to accept your generous offer."

"I have also asked Ian to secure you a mount. I know how accustomed you have become to your daily rides at Alverston, and I know Ian has a string of horses that are always in need of exercise."

"I hope Lord Umber will not consider it an encumbrance, for I do not wish him to think I am incapable of organizing my own divertissement," Felicia retorted more sharply than she intended and quickly added in a lighter tone when she saw the questioning expression in Lady Louisa's eyes. "What I meant to say was I do not want Lord Umber to feel obliged to escort me. I am certain he has better use for his time."

"I think I am the best judge of that, Miss Richards," Lord Umber said from the doorway. He bowed deeply. "Good evening, ladies."

Felicia cast him a furious look and wondered why it was he always had her at a disadvantage.

"Good evening, Ian," Lady Louisa answered. "I take it you have dined."

"Too well," he replied ruefully. "David has a fine chef."

"Do come in for a moment, my dear," Lady Louisa continued. "We were just talking about you."

"So I heard," Lord Umber said mildly. "Myself and horseflesh, I believe." He turned to Felicia. "I merely dropped by tonight to ask if you will give me the pleasure of your company tomorrow, Miss Richards. I declare I have discovered the prettiest little filly in my stables who is surely in need of a gallop."

Felicia felt his eyes mocking her, and she looked at him suspiciously. His conciliatory tone made her feel uneasy, but the temptation of riding in Hyde Park overcame her misgivings. "I will gladly accept, m'lord," she responded lightly. "Especially as Lady Louisa assures me that to be seen in your company will of a certainty increase my consequence."

Lord Umber gave a shout of laughter, and a smile lingered, softening the mockery in his eyes. "I will see you at ten sharp, then." He bowed as he wished them a good night, at the same time promising his mother he would accompany them both to the theater whenever she desired.

"Such a dutiful son," Lady Louisa breathed happily. "I am so fortunate." Felicia, not wanting to disagree, steered the conversation to safer ground.

The remainder of the evening was uneventful, and both retired early, so Felicia had no difficulty in presenting herself at the appointed time the following morning.

The ride was exhilarating, and Felicia found the ritual of the morning ride fascinating. The mild weather had brought out a crowd of strollers, and it seemed to her that all the women were trying to outdo one other with their ridiculous fashions.

"I have never seen such a silly parade of peahens," she

whispered to Lord Umber, as her gaze took in the scene. Then her eyes picked out the hobbling gyrations of a young dandy who was mincing his way toward a group of young ladies. "Whoever is that, m'lord," she inquired, her eyes dancing with mirth. "I swear I have never seen the like in my life. Those shoes! Oh! Dearie me!" Unable to hold her laughter a moment longer, she gathered her reins in and trotted away.

Lord Umber caught up with her and admonished her playfully. "Really, Miss Richards, you must learn to control yourself. Sir Ashbury holds himself in the highest regard and would be most displeased to learn that you are not swooning with admiration."

"So that is Sir Ashbury," Felicia said. "I recall some mention was made of him last week. Lady Philippa said his self-importance was as large as his fortune. I begin to see what she means."

They continued on along Rotten Row, commenting from time to time on various people. They were at ease, and Felicia was once again surprised at their harmony.

A discreet cough broke into their conversation, and Lord Umber started forward as he saw Lady Barbara waiting to speak to him. Her coachman had drawn up the barouche to one side of the carriage way, but even so it was blocking traffic.

"Good day, Lord Umber, Miss Richards," she said frostily. "A lovely morning for taking the air."

A few pleasantries were exchanged, neither party lingering, but they stayed long enough for Felicia to get the impression that Lady Barbara was angry at not being included in their party.

"It would seem that Lady Barbara is offended," she

said, her voice deceptively mild. She had not found much to like in Lady Barbara the previous week, although she herself had gone out of her way to be pleasant. Lady Barbara was a willful, spoilt creature, who was happy only when the conversation concerned her. Felicia had been amazed to learn that Lord Umber had set her up as his latest flirt and wondered whether his intentions were serious.

"You have stolen a march on her," Lord Umber replied immodestly. " 'Tis not something she is likely to forget or to forgive!"

"I do believe you are using me," Felicia retorted angrily. "You deliberately invited me to go riding with you today, knowing that Lady Barbara would be affronted when she saw us. Oh! You . . . you are unspeakable."

"But you do not let the fact that you are using me disturb you? Come, Miss Richards, let us act the part of friends, if only for the sake of appearance. It would not do your standing any good to be seen on the outs with me."

The very fact that he was justified in making his comment angered Felicia more. "I wish to go home," she said ungraciously, a tight smile barely creasing her face. "My thanks for parading me in front of the ton. 'Tis a pity no one recognized me."

They trotted home in silence and were soon in front of Lady Louisa's house. Before Felicia had time to dismount, Lord Umber was off his horse and by her side, forcing her to accept his assistance. He swung her easily to the ground and held her waist a few seconds longer than necessary before releasing her. "Am I forgiven?" he asked mischievously, as he smiled down at her. "For I swear I did not mean to offend you—only give Lady Barbara a setdown, for she has come to expect too much of me." Without waiting for an answer, he caught her hand and drew it towards his lips. "I shall look forward to escorting you to the theater." He kissed her hand briefly and before Felicia could reply, he was up on his horse and away, leading her mount behind him.

She was more shaken by his action than she cared to admit and looked down at her gloved hand in amazement. Shaking her head, she mounted the steps and entered the house.

"Is that you, Felicia?" Lady Louisa's voice floated into the hallway. "Hurry, child, I have need to speak to you."

Felicia ran into the blue drawing room, carefully removing her riding hat as she went. "Yes, Lady Louisa," she answered, stopping short as she saw the look of agitation on Lady Louisa's face. "Whatever is the matter, ma'am?"

"I have just heard from my friend in Manchester, Felicia. And she says there is no such person as Mrs. Barton, and the address you were given is nonexistent."

Eight

Dr. Ross had just seen the last patient in his waiting room when the messenger from Lady Louisa arrived. Her note was short, merely asking him to call at his earliest convenience, so he dismissed the messenger saying he would be there later that afternoon. He was not expecting Felicia to resume her treatments with him until the morrow, so he assumed Lady Louisa was inviting him for a social visit.

It was only when the second missive arrived an hour later from Lord Umber that he realized there was some urgency to the matter. Pushing aside the papers he was working on, he hurried out into the street and was thankful to see a vacant hackney on the corner. Ten minutes later he was being ushered into the small study at Lady Louisa's house. Lord Umber rose to greet him.

"Paul! Thank you for coming so promptly. It's Mama.

Nothing serious, I am sure, but she has had another attack of nerves." There was a worried note in Lord Umber's voice.

"I will go and see her immediately, Ian, but I don't think you need worry. I am certain it has been brought on by the excitement of seeing all her old friends. I rather suspected it might happen."

"Not Mama," Lord Umber smiled. "The attention she has been getting from all her old cronies has been most gratifying. No, she has just received word from her friend in Manchester, and it is that which has her overset."

"Miss Richards is to leave soon, then?"

"Far from it, Paul. It would appear that someone has played a malicious trick on the fair Miss Richards. There is no such person as her Mrs. Barton."

"No one!" Dr. Ross exclaimed. "Are you sure?"

"Absolutely. I have read the letter through umpteen times and there is no mistake. Here, read it for yourself."

Dr. Ross read the letter and was silent for a moment before asking, "How does Miss Richards feel about this?" There was a genuine note of concern to his voice.

"She took the news stoically enough, Mama said, but is now convinced that we will suppose she deliberately planned the entire gig."

"What utter nonsense!"

"My words exactly, Paul. But I am afraid that I have the strange ability to rile Miss Richards, and for reasons best known to herself, she delights in misunderstanding everything I say to her."

"Excuse me, then, Ian. I had best see both ladies and try to calm them. Mayhap I can persuade Miss Richards that we don't believe the worst. Though there is no denying that it is a setback for her. The question is, why would anyone want her out of the way?"

He left Lord Umber, shaking his head slowly. He was still shaking it when he returned.

"I just do not understand, Ian," he said. "It is the most callous trick to play on anyone."

"I am inclined to agree with you, Paul. How is she now?"

"Calmer. As you said, she has an amazingly prosaic attitude that enables her to bear tremendous stresses. She will come about, I have no doubt on that score. I am even hopeful that this may shock her into remembering something that will be useful. The mind works in such strange and deceptive ways, Ian, it is fascinating. Absolutely fascinating."

"Quite so, Paul," Lord Umber interrupted hurriedly, for he was in no mood to sit and listen to a dissertation on the therapeutic benefits of animal magnetism.

Dr. Ross smiled, as if he realized what was on his friend's mind. "Oh! By the way, I have persuaded her that the job as companion to Lady Louisa is as permanent as she wants it to be."

"Of course. How could it be otherwise? Did she accept?" His hidden anxiety was apparent to Dr. Ross as he asked the question. "At least Mama will be happy," he continued as the doctor nodded his head in agreement.

"It was the best possible news I could give Lady Louisa. She perked up immediately, though she is still a deal upset by the thought that Miss Richards might have been stranded in an alien city without friends or money. I would prescribe a quiet night for the pair of them, and they will be as right as rain in the morning."

"She . . . eh, Miss Richards. Did she indicate how long she wished to remain with Mama?"

"At least until we can discover who her family is. She is level-headed enough to realize that she cannot be wandering the streets without knowing who she is."

"I should think not," Lord Umber ejaculated. "Anyway, I would not let it happen. Does she say what she plans to do in the event her memory fails to return?"

"You mean, should I fail? That, my dear friend, is a word she does not accept, and I do believe I am beginning to share her optimism. You know how convinced I am that she is of a genteel background," he continued abruptly.

Lord Umber nodded, wondering what was on his friend's mind.

"I have asked Lady Louisa to make some inquiries through her friends about a family called Richards. Conceivably you could do the same, discreetly, of course?"

"You think we can turn up something to help you?"

"It is worth a try. I need hard facts to use when I have Miss Richards in a trance. I have still been unable to jolt her unconscious mind into recalling anything other than fragments of her happy childhood memories. I know I am on the verge of breaking through, but I need names and places that are familiar to her."

"I will bear it in mind, then, Paul," Lord Umber said as he pulled out his fob watch and opened it casually. "In fact, I can start immediately. I promised to look in at Lady Barbara's for tea, and there is bound to be a cluster of her admirers I can ask."

"Good, good," Dr. Ross said absent-mindedly. "I look forward to hearing from you."

However, it was Lady Louisa, on the following afternoon, who uncovered the first clue of Felicia's true heritage. They had arrived at Lady Jersey's imposing house in Belgrave Square at the appointed hour, and Lady Louisa was immediately surrounded by many of her old friends. Felicia managed to slip out of the circle without being missed and within a very few minutes had struck up a conversation with a shy, unimpressive young girl who looked pathetically out of place. Her chaperone was one of the women clamoring for Lady Louisa's attention.

Some time after their entrance, Lady Louisa managed to find a seat and, drawing one of her oldest friends, the Honorable Mrs. Melanie Courtney, out of the main press of people, bade her be seated. This was not a thoughtless gesture, for Melanie Courtney was known to be a walking Debrett's. Casual chatter composed the conversation for a while until Lady Louisa artfully brought up Felicia's name and quickly outlined the mishap that had befallen her with the resultant loss of memory.

"How terribly confusing for the poor child," Melanie murmured sympathetically, quizzing Felicia through her lorgnon. "And such a beauty, too. What a terrible shame. Your niece, you say, Louisa?"

"No. No, Melanie," Lady Louisa said hastily, for it would never do if that exaggeration was put around. "Great Aunt Agatha's granddaughter," she improvised quickly. "A very remote connection. But when I needed someone to make the journey with me, Great Aunt suggested Felicia, as she thought the change would be beneficial."

"So prettily behaved, too," Melanie continued approvingly. "I can quite see her capturing a few hearts this Season. Not a large fortune, I don't expect, if she is from Agatha's side."

Lady Louisa shook her head as she wondered what trouble her one lie would lead to.

Melanie, who had two sons of marriageable age, was in no way put out that another beauty had arrived on the scene. Her only regret was that Felicia did not have a large dowry. She sighed. What a pity that face and fortune seldom accompanied each other.

"Did you say you knew Felicia's mother, Melanie?" Lady Louisa asked vaguely, afraid that she had lost her friend's attention. "I never met her myself. She must have been in London during my confinement with Ian."

"Richards, you said, was the last name?" Melanie frowned in unaccustomed concentration. "I do believe I met Arabella once or twice, but that was years ago. 'Twas not the done thing at all, as I recall, to speak to her for she had eloped with a gambler. It was just a rumor, which I never did set much store by, of course . . . that he was a gambler, I mean. They dropped out of sight as he had supposedly won a small fortune from one of the York's. But you know how it was in those days, ladies were never included in any of the really interesting conversations. That didn't stop us from speculating though." She smiled at her own recollections.

"Of course," Lady Louisa agreed. She quickly took a sip of the tepid tea as the excitement she felt at uncovering the name of Felicia's mother threatened to overwhelm her. "Whatever became of Mr. Richards? Great Aunt always did refuse to talk about him."

Melanie's barely concealed yawn indicated she was getting bored with the topic. "Lord only knows," she answered carelessly. "As I said, they both vanished. Although, perhaps I did hear something to the effect that he was consumptive. Mayhap he died." She glanced around the room and espied another acquaintance of hers. "Aha! I see Lady Gordon has arrived. What a wretched hat she is wearing! You would think she would know better than to dress herself up in all those feathers."

Lady Louisa glanced toward the unfortunate lady in question. "I don't know, Melanie, dear. I think she looks quite becoming. Besides, feathers are so fashionable nowadays, even though they do make one sneeze." Disappointment at not being able to pursue her conversation about Felicia caused her to speak unthinkingly, and it was only when Melanie sniffed loudly and moved away, her voluminous taffeta underskirts rustling like a galleon in full sail, did Lady Louisa remember that one should never disagree with the Honorable Mrs. Courtney.

She sat back in reflective silence as she pondered Felicia's parents. Her instinctive reaction was to protect her from the truth, but she knew that was an impossibility. "Poor child," she murmured to herself. "I do hope she will be all right."

"Louisa!" Lady Jersey's voice boomed. "How absolutely divine you look! Positively radiant! Whatever made you stay away for so long? I swear you are a wonderful tonic to us all."

Lady Louisa smiled sweetly at Sally Jersey's friendly compliments, and pushed her meditations away. "Sally dear, it is so good to see you after such a long time. Though with your looks and vigor, you are in no need of a tonic. Nay, 'tis you that remind us that health and happiness go together. You make me feel quite ashamed for staying away for so long."

"Seriously, my dear Louisa, it is truly wonderful to have you back in our midst. I cannot tell you how much your gentle good humor has been missed. Without your restraining arm, we were turning into a bunch of savages."

"I am thankful I have returned in time, then, Sally," Lady Louisa laughed. "For I would hate to be thrust into the position of a missionary!"

"Who is the young lady you are chaperoning?" Lady Jersey asked abruptly. "Do I know the Richards family? A comely girl." She stared rudely at Felicia as she gave her voice of approval. "A credit to you. I suppose you are looking for vouchers?"

Lady Louisa nodded, glad that on this occasion Felicia was not within earshot. For she had been most adamant this morning about not wanting vouchers or any other such nonsense that would end up costing more than she could ever hope to repay.

"It would put me in your debt, Sally, for I know Felicia's sojourn in town would not be complete without a visit to Almack's. And I do hear talk that a certain young lady is in need of a little competition."

"Haven't changed a bit, have you, Louisa?" Lady Jersey laughed. "Still able to twist us all around your little finger and get us to do exactly what you want. Well, this time, it will be my pleasure. As you have so shrewdly observed, we could do with another beauty on the scene. Lady Barbara is in need of a setdown. She has become far too conceited, and the attentions of your son have only raised her expectations." Her voice was light as she teased Lady Louisa. "What is her pedigree, did you say?"

"I didn't, Sally, for you never gave me a chance! Great Aung Agatha. A remote connection, but a good one." She sent up another prayer for forgiveness for the lie, and hoped that when the truth came out her standing in Society would be sufficient for her to hold onto her position.

"I will send them to you then, Louisa," Lady Jersey said as she moved away, chuckling to herself. She always enjoyed Lady Louisa's company.

Felicia looked toward the awesome figure that was bearing down on them and curtsied when Lady Jersey introduced herself. After a few seconds of conversation, Felicia saw Lady Louisa beckoning to her so she excused herself thankfully and obeyed the summons.

"Enjoying yourself, child?" Lady Louisa asked indulgently. "Sally Jersey always has such interesting soirees, don't you think?"

"This one most certainly is, ma'am, but I cannot speak for the rest, as I have never attended one before."

"Who was that girl you were talking to? She seems to be a shy little thing. It was prodigious kind of you to sit with her so long. Even Lady Jersey remarked on it."

"That was Miss Williams. She has been sent up to London by her wicked stepmother to find a husband." Felicia rolled her eyes in mock horror. "And she is terrified of the fate in store for her should she return home without the necessary ring on her finger."

"You silly chit," Lady Louisa laughed. "With looks like that and no fortune, I fear the worse for her."

"That is unfair, ma'am." Felicia protested. "She does have a respectable dowry, and I swear with a change of hairstyle and a more becoming cut of clothes, she would do well enough. In fact, I have recommended she go to Miss Sophy."

"So kind of you, my dear," Lady Louisa murmured distractedly. She was already thinking of the note she wanted to write to Dr. Ross and was eager to get home. "But I do not think it necessary to take a more personal interest in her welfare. It would never do, my dear girl, for word to get around that you collect strays."

Felicia giggled. " 'Tis what people would accuse you of, ma'am, if they knew the truth about me. Miss Williams at least has an authentic pedigree."

"Quite so. Quite so," Lady Louisa rejoined unabashed. "But with me, people will put it down to mere eccentricity." She rose from her seat, dismissing the subject. "Come. I declare I am fagged to death and, as Ian has promised to join us for an early supper, I will need to rest a while. Say your good-byes prettily to Lady Jersey, for she has been prodigious generous."

Felicia looked at Lady Louisa blankly. "Generous, ma'am?"

"I will tell you more about that later," Lady Louisa said hastily. "Let us go before I find myself engaged in more exchanges of gossip."

They made their farewells and were soon ensconced in their carriage. Felicia looked out the window morosely as she felt her enjoyment of the afternoon slip away at the thought of Lord Umber's dining with them. The last thing she wanted was an intimate meal with him, for she was afraid that the mutual antagonism they felt for each other would not go unnoticed by Lady Louisa. Perhaps she could plead a headache and yet, she was anxious to find out how his affair with Lady Barbara was progressing. She sighed unhappily. Oh! How she wished she did not find his presence so disturbing. His arrogance always seemed to anger her even though David had told her that it was a veneer and something she should try to ignore. Her thoughts drifted to the friends of Lord Umber she had met, and she decided that David was certainly the most considerate. Dr. Ross she regarded in an entirely different light, though he was probably the closest friend of the Alverston family. Her relationship with him was entirely professional, hence it precluded personal feelings. Yet she knew instinctively that she could rely on him for help if she ever found herself in trouble.

She almost enjoyed her visits with him. The only thing to mar her pleasure was her inability to recall anything of importance to help him. In her many talks with him, she had discovered how dedicated he was to his mentor, Anton Mesmer, and how important solving her case had become. For Mesmer was experiencing difficulties in Vienna and Paris persuading people to believe in his methods for curing the sick. His reputation for effecting strange cures was arousing interest only with the occultists. Dr. Ross was convinced, however, that if it could be shown that serious students of medicine were able to effect similar cures using Mesmer's animal magnetism methods, then the professinal physicians and chemists might be more willing to listen and believe the practical evidence of his theories.

The opening of the coach door interrupted her reverie, and with an effort she shook off her depression. A note from Lord Umber was waiting, which the butler delivered to Lady Louisa on a silver platter. It merely informed his mother that David would be joining the party for dinner.

How typical of him, Felicia thought irritably, to invite more people without giving a second's thought to the inconvenience it would cause. Now it would be impossible for her to cry off, for she could not leave Lady Louisa to entertain both men by herself.

Lady Louisa was anxious to see her son alone, to apprise him of her findings. So she hurried through her toilette, much to the surprise of her maid, Lucy, and was downstairs waiting when her son's arrival was announced.

"I am so pleased that you are early for once, Ian," she said laughingly. "For I have need to speak to you alone."

Lord Umber bowed over his mother's hand gracefully, pleased to see her in such high spirits. "What is this?" he joked. "A long forgotten, deep, dark secret you want to divulge. Or gossip from Lady Jersey that you want me to confirm or deny?"

"Don't be such a goosehead, Ian, it's nothing of the kind." She paused dramatically. "I know who Felicia's parents are."

Lord Umber jerked back his head in surprise. "By Jove!" he exclaimed. "That is good news."

Lady Louisa shook her head dubiously. "I am none too certain about that, for I do not know whether they are dead or alive." Quickly she recounted what she had learned that afternoon.

"Perhaps Paul is right, then, Mama. Miss Richards' parents are of the first stare." He broke off as he heard the sound of approaching footsteps and looked toward the door. He was momentarily dazzled by the beauty he saw standing in the entrance and hesitated slightly before moving forward to greet Felicia.

"Miss Richards," he said, making an elegant leg. "I need not ask if you are well, for 'tis obvious that you are." His eyes strayed to her bosom, and he looked away quickly. The soft swelling of her breasts revealed by the low-cut dress was a tantalizing sight.

Felicia was conscious of his scrutiny. "Good evening, Lord Umber," she said somewhat breathlessly, acutely aware of his gaze and annoyed that she found his approving look pleasing. She turned away from the source of her confusion and smiled at Lady Louisa. "I am sorry to have kept you waiting," she murmured, "but Lucy took longer than I thought possible to do my hair."

"As the result is perfection," Lord Umber said huskily, "we will forgive you, won't we, Mama?"

The dinner surprised Felicia by being an extremely pleasant occasion. Lord Umber, looking resplendent in an ultrafine, close-fitting evening coat of the deepest shade of plum, set off to perfection by his champagne-colored pantaloons, went out of his way to be charming. Any restraint Felicia felt because of their last meeting quickly evaporated and by the time David arrived, a pleasing harmony had been achieved.

Lady Louisa looked on indulgently and was delighted to observe her son and David so obviously enjoying themselves. Felicia, positively glowing from all the attention, seemed well able to hold her own in such company. She sighed contentedly, pushing aside the only cloud in her mind—for she had already decided that Felicia's pedigree was good enough for her family, even though her father was a gambler.

Nine

Dr. Ross had cancelled all his appoint- ments, except for Felicia. He had a feeling that their next session would be long and productive. Felicia arrived on time, and within minutes he had put her in a deep trance.

"Tell me, Miss Richards," he asked, "does the name Arabella mean anything to you?"

"She is my mother," Felicia answered promptly.

"Then she is still alive?"

"Of course," Felicia replied.

"Where is she now?"

"At home with my father."

"And where is home?"

"In Hereford. We live in a small cottage . . . it is so pretty at this time of year. In summer the roses grow all around the front door . . ." Felicia paused for a moment as childhood memories flooded back. Even her voice took on a childish quality.

Dr. Ross sat back, barely able to contain the rising excitement he felt.

"Papa has to go away again, though," Felicia continued. "He . . . he says we need the money. I do wish he could stay at home, for Mama is so miserable when he is absent."

"What does he do when he leaves you and your mother?"

Felicia looked unseeingly at Dr. Ross. "I cannot remember. I don't know."

"He plays cards, doesn't he? He gambles for money in order to provide you and your mother with food?"

"I don't know," Felicia cried wildly. "It seems such a long time ago."

"Of course, you can remember, child, it is just that you don't want to."

"No. No. It's not true. Please say it's not true." Tears were streaming down her face by now and she was rolling her head from side to side in grief.

"Your papa never returned, did he?" The question was asked gently, but Felicia twisted unhappily on the striped Regency chair and continued to shake her head. It was as though she was trying to shake off some terrible thought. "But he must come back, he must. If not . . ." she broke off abruptly as a fit of sobbing overcame her.

"There, there, my dear," Dr. Ross soothed. "It's all over now, isn't it?"

Felicia nodded, her distress evaporating under the doctor's calm voice. "The man said he had been killed in a duel. I can see him now." She shuddered as the remembrance of that fateful day flooded back, and she started to cry again.

Dr. Ross took her hand in his and patted it. "I know how distressing it must be for you, Miss Richards, but if we are to get to the bottom of your trauma we must probe a little further. This man who came to tell you of your father's death. What is his name?"

"I cannot think," Felicia replied, her voice losing the childlike resonance. "He said he was only an acquaintance of Papa's. I have never seen him before."

"How did your father die?"

"The man said Papa had been shot by a fellow card player, after Papa had accused him of cheating." Felicia broke off again. "Why . . . why . . . did it have to happen to Papa? We were so happy."

Her storm of tears increased, and Dr. Ross gathered her into his arms and rocked her like a baby. "Try and calm yourself, Miss Richards. I think we have done enough for the moment. We will continue some other time." He kept his arms about her until she regained control of herself, and then he gently smoothed her hair back under her bonnet before releasing her.

Felicia sniffed loudly and gratefully accepted the large handkerchief he handed her. She blew her nose hard and then sat back and looked at the doctor questioningly. She was now quite obviously out of the trance. He rose from his chair and paced the room as he thought of the best way to discuss his findings with her. The exultation he felt at his remarkable breakthrough was difficult to suppress, for after the many fruitless sessions of the recent past, he had begun to doubt the validity of his experiment. Now, at last, he had broken through the wall of grief she had built up.

"What did you learn today, Dr. Ross?" Felicia asked hesitantly. It was unlike him to be so pensive. "How did I respond this time?"

Still he hesitated, and Felicia felt some alarm. "It is not good news then?" she asked flatly.

"My dear," Dr. Ross said, stopping at her side so that he could put his hand on her shoulder. "It is somewhat as we suspected. Your father is dead."

"And what of Mama?"

"We didn't get that far. I thought it best for you to take a rest. Your remembrances were somewhat upsetting."

Briefly, he outlined her recollections, and when he had finished, Felicia sprang out of her chair in agitation. "Poor Mama. Perhaps we can continue tomorrow, Dr. Ross, for I shall worry until I know whether she is all right. Maybe she is in need of me. Oh! How I wish I knew why I was on my way to Manchester."

Dr. Ross looked at her in amazement. Her selflessness was amazing. Even now, she was thinking of the discomfort her mother could be suffering—if she were still alive—instead of concerning herself with her own problems. "I know how you feel, Miss Richards, but I think it advisable to give you a few days rest to digest all this new information. This way, you may remember more on your own. Why not come and see me, say in two days' time."

"If you think so, Doctor," Felicia said doubtfully, "but I will be on your doorstep sooner, should I recall even the slightest thing."

Dr. Ross laughed. "Then I hope to see you tomorrow. Now, be off with you, and give my regards to Lady

Louisa and my apologies for being unable to join the theater party tomorrow."

Felicia picked up her pelisse and waited while Dr. Ross helped her into it. "Thank you, doctor," she said softly. "Thank you for everything." So my father was a gambler, she thought as she hailed a hansom cab. That would go a long way toward explaining her reaction to Cuthbert's disclosure that Lord Umber grew those wretched orchids for a bet. She pondered whether or not she should explain to Lord Umber but decided against it. Too much had been made of that incident already.

The visit to the theater was the first public engagement for Lady Louisa, and she insisted that Felicia wear her prettiest gown—a sapphire blue quilted silk, ornamented with a band of pale blue around the hem and the edge of the capped sleeves. The low, scalloped neckline revealed more of her bosom than Felicia deemed necessary, but Lady Louisa assured her it was the rage to be so daring.

"Really, Felicia my dear, if you wore it any higher, you would feel a positive dowd. There is nothing wrong with exposing a little of your charms."

Felicia thought of the night the duke came for dinner and remembered how his eyes had strayed to these "charms."

"But I feel naked," she complained, "and uncomfortable. Will not everyone stare at such daring?"

"Only at your beauty, my dear," Lady Louisa soothed. "Ah! That must be Ian now." She turned to her maid. "Just finish dressing Miss Richards' hair, Lucy. I will go on downstairs, for I have something to discuss with my son."

She left the room hastily, while Lucy fussed with Felicia. She smiled to herself at the dubious look on the child's face. Such modesty was quite charming.

"It's right, what ma'am says," Lucy said. "You 'ave a natural grace that most women would envy."

Felicia turned her head from the mirror to look directly at Lucy. "Thank you, Lucy, but I fear you are too generous with your compliments."

Lucy shrugged her shoulders in disagreement, but refrained from making further comment. It was a pleasure to work with such a kind person. Felicia was always so full of consideration.

Lady Louisa made her way to the drawing room swiftly. She had been concerned that Ian would resent forfeiting another evening of pleasure to escort them to the theater, but it was apparent that he was in the best of humors and actually enjoying himself.

"Good evening, Ian," Lady Louisa said prettily. "I hastened down ahead of Felicia to insure that you are not adverse to spending yet another evening in our frivolous company."

"Far from it, Mama," he answered smoothly. "I declare that I am quite looking forward to it. How is Miss Richards? Paul has told me the sad news."

"She will be glad when it is all over, I think. She is doing her best to conceal her worries about her mother but, quite honestly, Ian, I do not think she is still alive. Nobody I have spoken to can recall Arabella Richards, and surely if she were still alive someone would have run into her."

"Not necessarily, Mama," he said. "Especially if the family was in straitened circumstances. They probably lived quietly, out of the mainstream of any real social life."

"Well," Lady Louisa said, trying to shake off her feeling of despondency. "We must not let Felicia suspect we have been talking about her, for that would really overset her."

"Quite so, Mama, quite so. Maybe the play will create a timely diversion." His voice had softened imperceptibly, and Lady Louisa glanced at him quickly.

"Your consideration is much appreciated, Ian. I am sure one day Felicia will thank you herself."

Lord Umber laughed. "I doubt it, Mama. I suppose we are all doing what we can to help her, without expecting anything in return."

Lady Louisa tried to conceal her surprise at the feeling in her son's voice. Maybe her dream would come true. Quickly, she changed the subject, afraid that he would suspect the direction of her thoughts.

The short drive to Drury Lane was uneventful and they were soon seated comfortably in Lord Umber's permanent box. Lady Louisa nodded to several friends. She pointed out several other people to Felicia, and Lord Umber filled them in with all the latest *on dits*.

"Lordie me! Ian," Lady Louisa exclaimed at one point. "Is that Lord Davenport? My, my, how he has aged."

"He still likes to ogle pretty young girls though," Lord Umber joked. "I remember your telling me that he wore his heart on his sleeve for you, Mama." He turned to Felicia. "After Mama turned him down, he went into a sad decline, I am told, and swore he would never marry."

"And did he?" Felicia asked.

"No," Lord Umber replied, casting his eyes upward in simulated disbelief. "And all because of Mama!"

"Tut! Tut!" Lady Louisa blushed. "Do not remind me of my youthful indiscretions. And do not exaggerate the story, Ian. You will have Miss Richards thinking me a dreadful flirt."

Felicia laughed. "And I swear you have not changed a bit, ma'am."

"And I get the feeling that she never will," Lord Umber agreed.

But Lady Louisa's attention had been caught by a vulgar-looking woman in the lower section of the theater, who was staring up at Felicia. She seemed quite agitated and every now and then would bend over and talk excitedly to a pimple-faced girl seated next to her. Lady Louisa discreetly indicated the object of her interest to Lord Umber and raised her eyebrows in question.

Lord Umber shook his head slowly in answer to the unspoken query, for he had never seen the woman before. He looked quickly at Felicia and with an inexplicable sense of relief was pleased to note that she was unaware of the attention being paid her. Surprised that he should feel so protective toward her, he decided perversely that he would find out who the woman was. It was just possible, he thought, that she might know Felicia. Suddenly it seemed quite important for him to find out the truth of her background. He glanced urbanely at his mother and settled in his seat to watch the first act.

Lady Barbara, seated several boxes away, fumed inwardly as she realized that Lord Umber had not even seen her. She gave a snort of anger as she looked at Felicia's beautiful profile and then consoled herself with the thought that Lord Umber could not possibly be attracted to such insipid looks. It was well known that he preferred the more vibrant looks *she* possessed.

"Lord Umber is remiss in acknowledging you tonight, dear child," her mother observed sarcastically. "You have not said anything to offend him, I hope."

Lady Barbara bit her lip and lowered her long silky lashes as she avoided her mother's questioning eye. He must be snubbing her because of the disagreement they had had at tea the other day over her remark about Felicia. Maybe it would have been wiser not to have repeated a conversation of her mother's she had overheard, that Felicia was merely using Lady Louisa as her entree into Society. Cousin Milly had certainly implied her comment was out of turn.

"Well, child?" her mother asked sharply.

"No, Mama," Lady Barbara said hastily. "I can think of naught. Mayhap his distraction is caused by a loss at the gaming tables."

The curtain rose at that point, ending further interrogation by her mother, for which Lady Barbara was thankful. Presently she turned her attention to the players, but was so busy planning her next move to ensnarl Lord Umber that she did not hear a word.

At the intermission, Lord Umber excused himself. "I have just seen someone I must pay my respects to," he said, and nodded slightly as Lady Louisa tossed her head lightly in the direction of the woman.

Felicia, who had seen Lady Barbara waving in their direction, assumed it was she Lord Umber wanted to see and felt a momentary depression of her spirits. However, she returned the wave before turning to Lady Louisa to ask about one of the actors.

Once outside the box, Lord Umber walked quickly into the foyer and recognized without difficulty the vulgar woman. He made his way, unhurriedly, over to her and bowed deeply. "Excuse me for intruding on your privacy, ma'am," he said in a deceptively mild voice. "But I noticed you looking at the young girl who is seated in my box. . . ." He paused expectantly.

"What of it?" the woman snapped unpleasantly. "A cat can look at a queen, can't it?"

Somewhat taken aback by her unnecessary rudeness, Lord Umber raised his quizzing glass and looked at the woman and her charge disdainfully. He bowed slightly. "I am truly sorry to have bothered you, but I was merely wondering if you recognized the young lady in question. However, it is quite obvious I have made a mistake."

"Yes, you have, young man, for I don't recognize you nor her. And what is more, I do not like to be seen talking to strangers." She turned to the girl who had been standing in a bewildered silence during this exchange. "Come child, let us return to the safety of our seats."

Lord Umber stayed where he was, as he watched the two ladies pick their way through the crowd. His suspicions had been aroused by the woman's violent reaction to his question, and the snippet of conversation that floated back to him caused him to pursue them. He was certain he had heard the girl ask why they could not acknowledge Felicia.

Before he could reach them, he was stopped by David Burton. "I say, Ian," Mr. Burton said. "You look in a devil of a temper. What's amiss? Lady Barbara turned you down?"

The scowl that had caused Mr. Burton's remark vanished from Lord Umber's face as he greeted his friend. "Far from it, old boy. You know better than most I am not in that line. No, I have just had a very strange encounter. See that lady over there. No, not Mrs. Hardcastle, the one behind her in the puce. See, she has Miss Pimples at her side. Do you know her?"

Mr. Burton stared hard at the unlikely object of Lord Umber's interest. He was about to shake his head, when he changed the action to a slow nod. The hooked nose was familiar. "I do believe it is Lady Ormstead, and Miss Pimples as you so rudely called her, must be the daughter. Dreadful woman as I recall, garish and offensive with a tendency to be overbearing."

"You know her then?" There was a note of jubilation in Lord Umber's voice. "She has recognized Miss Richards but refuses to acknowledge her. What do you know of the woman?"

"Nothing intimate," Mr. Burton said quickly. "Are you certain that she knows Miss Richards?"

He listened in amazement as Lord Umber recounted the recent incident.

"How extraordinary," he exclaimed when Lord Umber had finished. "I have only met with Lady Ormstead a few times, for I did some legal work for her husband. In fact, the last time I went to see her was . . ." He paused, deep in thought. "When was Charles's house party?"

"Six months ago, at least," Lord Umber replied. "Why do you ask?"

"I visited Lady Ormstead at the same time. Ian . . .

Ian, my friend," Mr. Burton's voice had changed pitch, and Lord Umber felt the excitement it generated. "I've got it," his voice was triumphant. "There was a Mrs. Richards staying with Lady Ormstead. I am sure of it."

"Absolutely certain?" Lord Umber asked.

Mr. Burton nodded. "She sat in the background, while Lady Ormstead and I discussed some legal matters. Actually, I hardly remember her for she was so quiet. My only recollection is of a woman in her early forties. She must have been a beauty in her youth." He shrugged his shoulders. "I am sorry, Ian, but that is about all I can remember. I wish I could be more helpful."

Lord Umber clapped him on the shoulder. "It's enough for the present. I shall pay a call on this Lady Ormstead on the morrow and force her to tell me about Mrs. Richards. Maybe they are related in some way."

"It's possible," Mr. Burton agreed cautiously. He looked at his friend guardedly. It was most unlike him to display his excitement so openly. " 'Tis important then for you to discover Miss Richards' pedigree?" he questioned lightly.

"It's solving the mystery that gives me the pleasure," Lord Umber responded evasively, but even as he finished speaking he knew it to be untrue. David was far too perceptive, for his question had been entirely correct.

Seeing the slight discomfort he had caused his friend, Mr. Burton changed the topic. "I am due at White's later for a rubber or two with Paul. Do you want that I should mention this to him? It might be helpful for his next session with Miss Richards."

Lord Umber nodded thoughtfully. "Absolutely, David, for she is due at Paul's first thing in the morning."

They parted soon after. Upon returning to his box, Lord Umber adroitly persuaded Lady Louisa and Felicia to leave just before the end of the play on the pretext that by doing so they would beat the crowds to the restaurant. "The truth is, Mamá," he whispered, "I do not want Miss Richards to confront that awful woman yet."

Ten

Unbeknownest to either Lady Louisa or
Lord Umber, Felicia had seen the vulgar woman staring
at her. However, it wasn't until she was already in bed
that she recalled the incident. The face, or was it the grim-
ace, seemed vaguely familiar, but once again she could
not place it. She woke many times during the night as her
mind conjured up pictures that made no sense. Always
she seemed to be doing household chores—if it were not
large pails of water she was carrying up and down endless
flights of stairs, then she was bent over guttering candles,
darning sheets, or sewing fine lace petticoats. Once she
even heard herself calling for her mother, and when she
awoke her cheeks were wet with tears. By the time morning came, she felt stiff and tired. The dark rings under her
eyes gave her face a pinched look, and as she gazed at
herself in the mirror she frowned at the image she saw.

"Thank goodness I am to see Dr. Ross today," she said to her reflection. "Maybe he can help me put a name to the odious woman. She must be important to have bothered me so."

Her feeling of apprehension increased with the idea that today could well be the day for remembering everything. Something seemed sinister, and for the first time since her accident she felt afraid of knowing the truth. With an effort she pushed these sentiments aside and quickly completed her toilette. With all the time she had spent musing, she had left little for breakfast.

As she hurried downstairs, she was startled to see Lord Umber coming from his mother's room. He was certainly up beforetimes, she thought.

"Good morning, Lord Umber," she said quietly, not breaking her step. "I beg you excuse my haste, but I am late this morning."

"Not too late for breakfast, I hope," Lord Umber said more sharply than he intended, but the glimpse of the bleak, pinched look on her face filled him with concern.

"Indeed not. That is where I am headed this very minute." She continued down the stairs, wondering at his gentle tone. Well, he was always much nicer immediately after visiting his mother.

Lord Umber stood on the lower landing for several moments, looking in the direction of the breakfast parlor. What on earth had happened to cause that look on Felicia's face? The discreet coughing of the butler recalled him to his surroundings.

"Will you be partaking of breakfast, m'lord?"

"What a splendid idea, Sims. I do believe I will." He entered the parlor and motioned Felicia to remain seated.

"You don't object to my joining you, Miss Richards?" he asked, helping himself to some eggs and kidneys that were being kept warm on the sideboard.

"It would do me little good to say yes," Felicia said lightly, as she looked meaningfully at his filled plate. "For where would you go with that?" In truth, she was thankful for the diversion, even though she had to contend with the sudden, heavy thumping of her heart that his presence caused. *Whatever is the matter with me?* she asked herself. *I am acting like a child just out of a nursery. It must be because I am overtired.*

"I am sure Sims would solve that dilemma," Lord Umbe replied, matching her light tone, in spite of the deepening concern he felt. Now, in the harsh daylight of the room, he could see the dark rings under her eyes, and the way she was toying with her food indicated that something was bothering her.

"In that case, sir, pray be seated, for I hesitate to put Sims to any extra trouble." She smiled as she spoke, and for just a moment their eyes held in a deep look.

A little shaken by the intensity of his feelings, Lord Umber quickly sat down. "Such kindness, Miss Richards, will not go unrewarded," he murmured, breaking the heavy silence that had developed.

They continued eating for a while, Felicia struggling to regain control of herself. The emotions she had just experienced alarmed her, although she realized that her sleepless night had a lot to do with her inability to be more calm.

"Is something the matter, Miss Richards? You do not seem to be in your usual spirits this morning."

"And pray what are they, sir? As this is only the second time we have met so early, you must surely realize that, like everyone else, I am a bad-tempered shrew until the afternoon."

Lord Umber forced a laugh, hiding his disappointment that she was unwilling to confide in him. He knew his reaction was foolish, even so he wished he could persuade her to trust him. "I am thankful to have escaped your more choleric disposition thus far then. In sooth, there is nothing more tiring than being black-browed before nuncheon."

Felicia lapsed into silence again, her thoughts on the woman in her dreams. She was tempted to ask Lord Umber if he had noticed her last night, but something held her back. Perhaps, if Dr. Ross was unable to help, then she would broach the subject with him.

"Miss Richards . . ." Lord Umber began, but was interrupted by Sims, who chose that moment to enter the room. He made his majestic way to the table and presented Lord Umber with a silver salver upon which reposed a letter. Lord Umber took it and opened it with some annoyance. His annoyance increased as he read the contents and a dark scowl settled on his handsome features.

"Not more bad news?" Felicia asked anxiously.

"No . . . no. Merely a note from Lady Barbara."

His tone discouraged further comment, but Felicia, glad that the subject of conversation had moved away from herself, continued, "I can guess at the message, for even Lady Lousia was moved to comment on the snub you delivered her last night."

"Mama? I wonder she noticed anything outside of her friends and what they were wearing." Why should his mother have made such a remark, he wondered, unless it was to divert Felicia's attention from Lady Ormstead. "But no, 'tis not as you suspect."

Felicia, aware that her inquisitiveness was both bad-mannered and unladylike, blushed. She could not deny that she had felt highly gratified when Lord Umber had seemed to deliberately ignore Lady Barbara, nor could she deny her curiosity over the note this morning. "I must apologize for my vulgar curiosity," she said quickly, "for I know it is not my concern. Now, if you will excuse me, I must go to keep my appointment with Dr. Ross."

"Of course," Lord Umber replied blandly, hiding his amusement at Felicia's ill-concealed interest in his affair with Lady Barbara. "I will accompany you, for I too have an early assignation. As to the other question, it would appear that Lady Barbara has been suffering an indisposition, which she feels goes a long way toward explaining why she has been out of sorts of late. 'Not her usual self,' is the way she puts it."

"You mean there is another side to her?" Felicia asked involuntarily, regretting her words immediately. "I mean, ah . . . ah . . . nothing serious, I hope?" *Why does my tongue always run away with me?* she thought miserably. *But, at least that explains his annoyance. With such a determined lady in pursuit, he must feel like a hunted animal. Still, there was no denying that he had brought it on himself, for there was no doubt he had encouraged her dreadfully.*

Watching the changing emotions race across her face, Lord Umber tactfully addressed himself to her second question. "No, I don't think it is anything serious. Although she didn't actually say what it is that ails her, she made mention that she was at home to visitors." He caught the disapproving, yet questioning look that Felicia threw at him and smilingly shook his head. "And, no, that is not where I am off to."

Put to the blush again, Felicia lowered her gaze, "I . . . I . . ."

"I think you should put my mother's mind to rest," he interrupted hastily. "The truth is, Miss Richards, I am at the devil's end to know how I can dissuade Lady Barbara from attaching too much importance to the times I have sought her out in company. It is now apparent to me that she cannot conceive the possibility she is not the uppermost thought in everyone's mind, especially mine. I am sure that she has received great encouragement from her mother, but Lord knows, I have done nothing to encourage her to think that my intentions were serious. Indeed, perhaps you can offer some advice." He lapsed into silence. *Now, why on earth did I use my mother as an excuse to reassure Felicia that Lady Barbara means nothing to me,* he wondered. *I must have taken leave of my senses.*

"Some advice, my Lord! How can I possibly advise you? And . . . and . . . just think how Lady Barbara would feel if she knew she was under this sort of discussion. I . . . I cannot possibly help you."

Unabashed by the outrage in her voice, Lord Umber sought to steer the conversation into lighter channels. Whatever impulse had propelled him to say what he had, was gone. "My dear Miss Richards," he cajoled, a merry twinkle lighting his eyes. "Her adage has always been 'I care not what anyone says, so long as they say it about me.' So I hardly think she would be overcome by the knowledge of our conversation."

"Lord Umber," Felicia said severely, trying hard not to let him see her amusement at his quip, "enough! I think I know you sufficiently well to believe you will find a solution to the dilemma you now find yourself in. After all, no matter what you may think, it is of your own making."

He chuckled. "Touché, Miss Richards. But if you do happen to think of anything . . ." he continued irrepressibly. "Shall we go?"

Felicia was still slightly bewildered by the conversation as Lord Umber swung himself into the coach and sat beside her. She would like to put it down to what Lady Louisa termed the "early morning syndrome," in which things were said or discussed by people whose brains were still asleep. But her own forwardness had gone a long way to encouraging such impropriety. There was no denying that Lady Louisa would be pleased to learn that her son had no intention of making his relationship with Lady Barbara permanent, and she had to confess that the news was welcome to her as well. Surreptitiously she stole a look at the impressive profile Lord Umber presented her, and let out a tiny sigh. She would definitely miss his presence when the time came for her to leave, for she could not refute the simple fact that she gained enormous comfort from the self-confident air that exuded from him.

"Are you uncomfortable?" Lord Umber asked, for he had heard the sigh.

"No. That would be an impossibility in such a well-sprung coach. I was trying to perform the difficult task of marshaling my thoughts for Dr. Ross."

"Do you find your sessions with him difficult?" He

watched her closely as she answered. The idea that it could be this that caused her sleepless night crossed his mind.

"Actually, I rather enjoy them. My only concern is that I take up too much of the good doctor's time."

Satisfied with her response, Lord Umber wondered again what it was that was troubling her. It was too late to probe further for the coach came to a halt. "Don't you worry about that," he said gently. "Just remember that Dr. Ross is enjoying every second of his experiment." He picked up her hand, squeezed it lightly. "Good luck, and I hope you give yourself some good news this time." He released her hand as the footman opened the door, and Felicia murmuring something unintelligible, disappeared into Dr. Ross's office.

Lord Umber sat back for the short ride to Lady Ormstead's house and contemplated the upcoming interview. It would be extremely interesting to hear what the woman had to say. Maybe she could even shed some light on Felicia's mysterious trip to Manchester, for that was the one truly puzzling aspect of the whole perplexing case. The woman's attitude last night was most peculiar and supported his theory that she was trying to hide something. Why else would she behave so suspiciously?

He had his secretary to thank for tracking down the whereabouts of Lady Ormstead. That priceless bundle of efficiency had spent a fruitless hour searching for her name in *Who's Who,* but finally succeeded when one of the undermaids confessed that her sister had, until recently, been in the employ of that "awful woman." Lord Umber marveled at his secretary's ingenuity, for he knew it would never have occurred to him to ask the servants.

Yet, now, on reflection, it was the most obvious thing to do.

The address was in a less fashionable thoroughfare of London, and as the coachman swung into Upper Grosvenor Street, Lord Umber was hard put to recognize the area. When the coach came to rest outside an unimposing, slightly shabby house, he wondered if perhaps his secretary had made a mistake. His doubts increased as he waited for someone to respond to his energetic hammering of the knocker and almost gave up in despair, when his summons was not immediately answered. Just as he was descending the steps, he heard the sound of chains being removed and so returned to wait impatiently for the door to be opened.

After what seemed to be mighty struggle with a bolt, the door was indeed opened, and a rumpled looking footman inquired if he could help.

"Indeed," Lord Umber said haughtily. "You can confirm that this is the residence of Lady Ormstead." He cast a look of disdain in the direction of the footman. Never had he seen such a slovenly servant.

"Yes, sir, m'lord. But she ain't at 'ome," the footman answered nervously, looking over his shoulder into the inky blackness of the house interior.

Lord Umber looked at him suspiciously, for it seemed unlikely that anyone had left the house that morning since the chains had still been in place until his arrival.

"Ah! I see," he said sarcastically, "the neighborhood is sufficiently unsafe to warrant keeping the door bolted at all times."

The footman looked uncomfortable as he nodded dumbly.

"Well, be so good as to take my card, young man, and make sure you tell Lady Ormstead that I shall return at 3 o'clock precisely, this afternoon." He took out his wallet with a flourish and removed a heavily embossed calling card which he placed very deliberately into the outstretched, trembling hand of the servant. Without waiting for a reply, he turned on his heel and was in his coach before the gaping footman could discharge the rest of the instructions Lady Ormstead had given him.

Slowly the footman closed the door and dragging his feet, made his way into the nether regions. When asked by the butler if he had said all the necessary, he shook his head.

"Didn't 'ave a chance. 'E was gone afore I could say Bob's my uncle. Said e'd be back this afternoon."

"You utter imbecile," the butler shouted, venting his spleen on the unfortunate underling. "I've a good mind to send you to Lady Ormstead to explain your stupidity."

"M . . . m . . . me, Mr. Nestor. I 'ardly think so, if you don't mind. 'Erself wouldn't listen to the likes of me."

Mr. Nestor gave him a stony look. "Enough of your impudence. Just make sure you deliver the entire message when Lord Umber returns." He left the quaking footman to answer the impatient ringing of Lady Ormstead's bell.

Lady Ormstead listened to Nestor in a distracted silence, merely commanding him to insure that her orders were carried out properly that afternoon. Her thoughts were on Felicia as she wondered what had happened to allow that scheming wretch to wriggle her way into such illustrious company. How had her carefully laid plans of losing Felicia in Manchester been overset. She had been so certain of success. Now she would have to think up another scheme.

Lord Umber gave way to his rising anger as his coach pulled away from Upper Berkeley Street. Never, never, had he experienced such rude or sloppy behavior. And, as if that wasn't insulting enough, to have to listen to such an obvious lie. Of course, the woman was in, but why was she so intent on avoiding him? The more he thought about it, the more convinced he became that she held the key to Felicia's identity. Suppressing his annoyance, he vowed that he would force an interview with Lady Ormstead that afternoon, no matter what obstacle she put in his way.

Abruptly he ordered his coachman to drop him at White's, for he suddenly wished for civilized company and conversation. He felt as though cobwebs draped his brain and that his preoccupation with Felicia's predicament was becoming an obsession. He had neglected so many things since his mother had been in town, including the delicious widow, Janie Slagle. It was high time he got on with his life and he vowed that after today he would expend his energy in that direction.

Eleven

The door closed behind Felicia with a thump as she stood in the entrance way. Her hand still felt warm from Lord Umber's clasp, and she put it to her cheek. *Enough of this nonsense,* she whispered to herself crossly. *I must not attach any importance to his actions, for I know they are prompted by pity.* She shrugged her shoulders and went forward to greet Dr. Ross.

Very quickly she told him of her dreams the previous night and waited expectantly for him to put her into a trance.

"I think I can clear up that mystery for you, Miss Richards," he said, deliberately deviating from the usual pattern he followed with Felicia. "Lord Umber saw the woman you are talking about, too, and discovered that her name is Lady Ormstead. Does this name hold any significance for you?"

132

Felicia stared at him and repeated the name to herself in a strangled whisper. "No! No! It cannot be. Please say it is not so, doctor." She jumped up from her seat and paced the room in agitation.

He tried to survey her calmly, but the realization that he had at long last broken through without the device of the trance caused an excitement that was almost too great to suppress. "Sit down, Miss Richards," he said quickly, "and let us try to sort this out. Why does the name upset you so? Who is this Lady Ormstead?"

Felicia didn't answer. Instead she clenched and unclenched her fists, only pausing in her pacing long enough to cast Dr. Ross a look of naked despair. Without warning she sank down on her knees and covered her face with her hands. The screams started as a low moan that seemed to come from deep within her, but by the time Dr. Ross had reached her side, they were agonizingly loud. Very gently he lifted her to an upright position, chiding himself for not recognizing her symptoms of hysteria sooner. No doubt the feeling of triumph he had just experienced had blinded him momentarily.

She continued to scream until he brought his hand down sharply across her face. Stunned into silence, she stared at him helplessly and then sagged against him limply. All color had fled her cheeks except for the scarlet lines his fingers had left.

"Your memory has returned, hasn't it, Miss Richards?" His voice was carefully controlled. He did not want to frighten her further, yet he knew that he must encourage her to speak before fear once again erased her memory.

"I remember everything. Everything. It's so awful. Dr. Ross, whatever am I going to do. She was trying to get rid of me. She deliberately sent me to Manchester, knowing there was no position. Why, why, would she be so cruel?" Felicia broke off, suddenly aware of the position she was in. Immediately, Dr. Ross released his hold on her and helped her up, steadying her with an arm.

"I have no answers for you yet, Miss Richards. If you have the strength we can continue discussing not only Lady Ormstead, but the events that led to your obvious fear of the woman." He led her to a chair and pushed her down into it. "Who is she?"

Felicia took time to compose herself before answering, and by the time she looked up at Dr. Ross an anguished look was chiseled into her face that made him swear softly to himself. "Lady Ormstead is my aunt." Her voice was devoid of expression.

It was now Dr. Ross' turn to pace. What a price this young girl had had to pay for his success! By rights he should feel elated for having successfully merged her conscious state with her unconscious mind. Undoubtedly, Mesmer and his colleague Nicolas Bergasse would, when he sent them his papers. His problem was he had allowed himself to become too involved, too close to the patient, for he now felt afraid for her and what the future held as the enormity of her disclosure struck him. "Do you want to tell me everything, as you remember it, or would you prefer that I put you in a trance? I do not want you suffering any more than necessary."

"I shall be all right, doctor, once I have grown used to the idea that my only living relative sought to 'lose' me in Manchester." She wrenched her mouth into a semblance of a smile. "The only mystery that remains in my mind is why she would want to do such a thing."

Dr. Ross turned away from her and went over to a decanter that was set on a side table. Quickly he poured some of the amber liquid into a glass and handed it to Felicia. "Here, Miss Richards, drink this down before you begin your story, it will help steady your nerves."

She smelt the liquid and pulled a wry face.

"It is only a drop of brandy and is very good medicine. Come, don't worry that you will feel lightheaded, for as you can see I have given you only a drop."

Felicia tossed the drink back and coughed as the fiery water burned its way down her throat. She gulped rapidly several times in a futile attempt to inhale some air. "Oh! Dearie me," she gasped.

"Now, drink this water," Dr. Ross continued, "and you will feel much better."

She accepted the glass gratefully and swallowed the water greedily. Closing her eyes, she leaned her head back and felt the churning in her stomach subside. She placed a hand wearily on her forehead and massaged her brow thoughtfully. "I am finding it difficult to know where to begin," she said finally, "for there is really so little to tell." She opened her eyes and smiled forlornly at Dr. Ross. "What would you like to know first?"

He looked at her sympathetically, for he knew there was nothing more he could do to help her except ask questions that would ease her back into the past. "I take it, from what you said earlier, that your mother is no longer alive?"

Felicia nodded sadly. "She died a few months ago. The doctor said it was due to a lung infection, but I believe now that Mama had lost her will to live." She glanced at Dr. Ross tentatively and at his smile of encouragement, continued. "After my father was killed, we were forced to seek my aunt's assistance. It was that, or the poorhouse."

"There were no other relatives to help you?"

"None that I knew of," Felicia answered, shaking her head. "You see, my parents eloped and that caused a terrible rift between them and their families which never healed. I do not know who my father's parents were—indeed they may still be alive—for Papa never spoke of them. Mama once said he was the younger son of an influential family, and after they married, they changed their name to Richards so as not to cause any further embarrassment to Papa's family. I do not even know Papa's true name."

"What of your mother's parents?"

"They died when Mama was a baby. She and Aunt Gweneth lived with an un̶c̶l̶e̶ and from the little mama let slip about him, he sounded like a tartar."

"So Lady Ormstead is your mother's sister?"

"Yes, Aunt Gweneth is Mama's older sister. I never met her until . . . until . . . we were forced to live with her, for like Papa, Mama never mentioned her immediate family."

Dr. Ross noticed the faraway look returning to Felicia's face and remarked quickly, "Your parents must have been very much in love to have endured such hardships."

"They were. Mama always said she never regretted running away." A more animated expression lit her eyes. "We were all so happy, except when Papa had to go away." Her face clouded over briefly at the remembrance of those infrequent trips to London. "But, otherwise, the lack of money never seemed a problem when we were together. And Papa used to earn money playing the piano, and he gave lessons to the children at the manor for a while. Everyone who heard him play said that with more training he would have become famous."

"Your father taught you as well, I presume?"

"That was the one luxury we allowed ourselves, a grand piano." She smiled suddenly, and Dr. Ross felt the warmth of it from where he was seated. "If you could have seen it, squashed into the largest room of the cottage we rented, you would have laughed. It looked so ridiculous. It didn't bother us though, as we all loved to play. Oh! They were such happy days. And the villagers were so kind, insisting on paying for the herbal brews that Mama concocted that eased all manner of aches and pains. She really was very knowledgeable about the medicinal use of plants."

"What happened after your father died?"

Abruptly, Felicia's expression changed, and a look of pain came over her eyes. "We could not afford to live on the money Mama made, so we sold the piano and what furniture we had to pay for the coach fare to Chepstow. Mama was too proud to ask Aunt Gweneth to send us the tickets."

"How long ago was that?"

"Nearly six years. That also explains why my playing is so poor, for until I met Lady Louisa I didn't play. Aunt Gweneth wouldn't allow anyone near her piano except Wendy."

There was a note of resignation to her voice that caused Dr. Ross to exclaim, "What a dreadful woman she sounds! Why don't you tell me about her, Miss Richards, for I can see quite clearly now that she is the true cause of your amnesia. The last six years of your life were the ones you were really trying to forget."

"They were awful years," Felicia agreed, thankful for his uncanny ability to interpret her fears. "After the serenity of Herefordshire, living at Graystones was a nightmare. Mama and I worked for our keep because Aunt Gweneth said she couldn't really afford to keep us as ornaments." A harsh and bitter laugh escaped her. "Mama worked from early morning to dusk in the sewing room and I was given the responsibility of looking after my cousin Wendy and Aunt Gweneth." The awfulness of those years came back to her in a rush. How could she ever have forgotten her aunt's cruelty? The delight she had taken chastising her in front of visitors for something left undone. And those friends—like Aunt Gweneth—frustrated, aging widows who enjoyed, nay relished, the punishment meted out.

Felicia shuddered at her recollections. How stupid she must have been not to have realized it sooner, but it now seemed apparent that her aunt had deliberately set out to break both her and her mother's spirit. The failure to break hers might well have goaded Aunt Gweneth into sending her to Manchester. And to think, but for the coach accident, she would have been totally alone in a strange city, without friends and with only a few guineas. Whatever would have happened if Lord Umber had not decided to rescue her. *Oh! Aunt Gweneth,* she cried inwardly, *I never realized you hated me so much.* Her thoughts returned to Lord Umber and his early, improper suggestion for her future. Maybe she should have accepted his offer, for now the future, as far as she could see, held very little.

"We can see where your dreams came from last night," Dr. Ross's measured tones interrupted her reverie. "Can you not recall anything at all that would explain your aunt's behavior toward you and your mother? Such heartlessness, in my experience, is usually based on some deep-rooted fear like jealousy or inferiority."

Felicia thought for a while before remembering the conversation her mother and aunt had had the day they arrived at Graystones. "There was just one conversation, when my aunt talked about Papa, but I am sure that it is not important."

"Let me be the judge of that, Miss Richards. Don't forget that every little fragment counts when you are trying to repair a shattered glass, and that is how I regard your mind. You have been through a grueling time and your memory cracked a little. To repair it completely we must find all the tiny pieces and put them back together."

Felicia smiled at his analogy. "You make so much sense, Doctor, if only I could think in such logical terms I would be able to stick myself together without any help at all."

Dr. Ross laughed, and his admiration for her courage and composure increased. "Now, what was this conversation?"

"It happened the day we arrived at my aunt's. I remember Aunt Gweneth sneering at Mama. Berating her for marrying a wastrel. She said that we deserved everything we got, and that, frankly, she was surprised we hadn't ended up in the poorhouse sooner. I know Mama did her best to defend Papa, but she was simply no match for Aunt Gweneth's tongue. Except she did say one thing that quieted Aunt Gweneth for a full minute." Felicia frowned as she tried to recall it exactly. "She said, 'you never could accept the fact that Andrew wanted to marry me, could you? You always thought it was you he preferred. I often wondered how you reacted when you found out that I had run off with the man we both wanted. Well, no matter what course your revenge takes, Gweneth, you will never be able to take away my memories, for they are happy ones.' After a few moments, my aunt started to scream, 'Happy! Happy! That is hardly the case now, is it, dear sister? Nowhere to go, no money to meet your debts. You come sniveling to me to take you and your brat in, and provide for you both. I have a good mind to turn you out and let you starve.' It seems to me, Doctor, that after that my mother lost her courage and begged Aunt Gweneth not to turn us away."

"What you have just told me, Miss Richards, is enough to convince me that your aunt is a highly disturbed person. I would advise you to try and forget the misery she forced on you and do your best to remember the happy times you had when your parents were alive."

"I will take any advice you have to offer, Doctor, except if you suggest that I return to my aunt. That is something I will never do."

"And you can rest assured that that is something I will never recommend."

Turning a limpid, trusting gaze on Dr. Ross, Felicia said, "Perhaps you can help me find employment?"

Startled by the unexpected question, Dr. Ross frowned. "Whatever do you mean? You are employed."

"Don't you see that I cannot continue working for Lady Louisa? Now that I know who I am, I must get used to the fact that I have to make my own way in the world. I cannot accept such generosity . . . it . . . it is not seemly."

Dr. Ross eyed her shrewdly. It could not be plainer if she had told him, for her feelings were etched on her face. The chit was in love with Ian. Lordie me, he thought, what a mix-up it is, especially as I doubt she realizes that that is her reason for running away. Unconsciously, she must feel her background is inferior. An unprofessional feeling of concern touched him as he realized how much her happiness meant to him. She appeared as fragile as a tiny bird who cried out for protection, yet underneath there was a self-reliant streak that refused to bend or be compromised. He wished he had more to offer her than advice, but to do so would be unfair and totally unprofessional. And, on reflection, she was right in wanting to put distance between herself and Ian, for if she stayed with Lady Louisa she would suffer every minute of every day.

Felicia surprised even herself when she asked Dr. Ross for his help, and now, in view of his long silence she was afraid she had somehow given offence. "Will you not help me?" she asked again.

"Yes, Miss Richards, I do believe I will, even though Lady Louisa will never forgive me."

"Oh! Thank you! Thank you!" Felicia cried in relief. "I knew you would not let me down."

"I will need a few days to make some inquiries, but I am certain that I shall be able to find you a comfortable position with one of my patients." Any misgivings he felt were eradicated by the look of pleasure Felicia gave him. "However, you must inform Lady Louisa of your plans, for my primary concern is still with her health."

"Of course, Dr. Ross," Felicia said quickly. "I am sure she will understand. I mean, she cannot possibly expect me to stay forever, and it is best for everyone if I go now before we become too accustomed to one another." The truth was, the prospect of the upcoming interview was daunting, for Felicia knew Lady Louisa would not accept her decision happily. It is for my own good, anyway, she reminded herself. If I stayed with her much longer, I would come to regard that style of living as my own, and that would never do. "And, another reason, Doctor," she continued lightly, "for my going, is that now that Aunt Gweneth knows where I am, she may plan something even more dreadful than a trip to Manchester."

"I hardly think she will be given the chance, Miss Richards. Not if I know Ian. It is my opinion that he will deal with her in such a way that you need never give her another thought."

"Whatever makes you suppose that Lord Umber would put himself about on my account? Is it because he regards me as one of his 'charities'?"

There was a pain in her voice that saddened Dr. Ross, and he hastened to comfort her. "I don't think so. Ian is a perpetual defender of the wronged and cheated, and there is no doubt that you have been cheated out of your rightful heritage and savagely wronged by a vindictive aunt. Lady Ormstead is the sort of bully Ian enjoys tearing down. It is also a small way he can repay the debt he feels he owes you."

"Debt? What debt are you speaking of?"

"The happiness you have brought his mother. You would find it difficult to believe the improvement your short stay has wrought in her. But I do assure you, Miss Richards, that before you arrived, we, all of us, had all but given up hope that she would ever rally her spirits.

The effect on Ian was equally bad, for the depression he experienced over his mother's imagined illnesses sent him hell-bent on his own destruction. He is a highly complex person and almost always manages to hide his true feelings under a flippant façade, but in many ways you have been responsible for both their recoveries."

Felicia looked at the doctor thoughtfully. She was not surprised by his words, for she had sensed much of what he was saying herself. There had been those few occasions when she had seen Lord Umber lower his guard, when she had glimpsed the considerate, sensitive person he strove to hide behind an inscrutable mien. Even so, she was positive of one thing, and that was she did not want to be at his mercy, especially when he was at his arrogant worst.

"Now remember one thing," Dr. Ross was saying. "I shall be here should you need me for anything. So do not hesitate to come and see me. In the meantime, I want you to enjoy your last few days with Lady Louisa as best you can, and not be worrying yourself over the rights and wrongs of taking charity, because you are not. Is that much clear?"

"Perfectly, Doctor," Felicia responded demurely. "And I will do my utmost to follow your orders. One other thing, though . . . I think I would prefer it if you would not tell Lord Umber or Lady Louisa about my past. I do not think I could bear their pity as well as everything else. It would make my last few days even more miserable."

"But, Miss Richards," Dr. Ross protested, "Ian will think it very odd of me to suddenly refuse to talk of the most important experiment I have yet conducted."

"You can discuss my case, all I ask is that you do not

disclose my family background, for if Lord Umber is half as meddlesome as I suspect he is, he could well be tempted to search out my real family name. Anyway, I cannot see why it should be necessary for either of them to know all the details. My memories are too painful."

"I shall respect your request, be assured of that." Proud to the end, he thought admiringly.

Twelve

When Felicia left Dr. Ross's office, she decided to walk for a while rather than get a hansom cab immediately. She had too much information to digest— too much to think about for the memories that were hammering at the inside of her head were making her feel quite dizzy. She also knew that if she were to face Lady Louisa with any equilibrium, her thoughts had to be sorted out immediately. It was going to be extremely difficult to explain to Lady Louisa her plan to seek employment elsewhere, so she would have to be careful how she approached it. One thing was certain, however, and that was she knew no arguments would be strong enough to persuade her to change her mind.

How could she stay and take advantage of Lady Louisa's hospitality when there was no hope of her ever being able to repay it? No, it was far better that she go now. And Lord Umber, he was another reason. His presence was far too disturbing. His image passed through her mind, and she hugged it to herself.

She paused at the curbside, crossing the cobble street before unwittingly taking a smaller side street. What hold did he have on her? For suddenly she could not deny that he was the real reason for her decision to start a new life. Did she dislike him that much? No. She knew that was not the case, for she was too honest not to admit that she enjoyed talking to him—even though they did not agree on everything. But she did find his presence invigorating and his conversation stimulated her mind. In fact, she always looked forward to seeing him.

She stopped abruptly as the truth hit her. She loved him!

Heedless of where she was going, Felicia kept on walking, unconsciously threading her way in and out of dray carts, horses, and merchants. How utterly foolish she had been not to have recognized her feelings for him sooner. No wonder her heart had thumped so painfully every time he had approached. No wonder she had felt so contemptuous of Lady Barbara—or had that been jealousy?

How blind you have been, she whispered as the realization of her true feelings toward Lord Umber overwhelmed her. *And how utterly stupid.*

Her aunt's behavior and the fact that she herself was an orphan paled into insignificance, as she tried to adjust to this more overpowering discovery.

Oh! I almost wish I had accepted the very first proposal he made me, she sighed. *At least I would have had some pleasant memories. . . . Is that a terribly shocking thought, Mama?* she asked, blushing at her own forwardness.

The memory of the embrace he had given her returned, and she arched her shoulders as though he were caressing her again. Would she ever forget the way his smile had caused creases to form around his eyes, and the way he had worn his hair—so carelessly tied back, yet so fashionable. And the gentleness he showed toward his mother. There were so many things about him that she loved. Well, she must not dwell on what might have been. Far better to put her daydreaming to one side, at least until she had found other employment, for it would never do for Lord Umber to guess the truth. She could well imagine the contempt he would feel if he discovered the romantic turn her thoughts had taken. His reaction to Lady Barbara was example enough, and she could not bear the thought that he would discuss her with someone else in similar fashion.

It would be as well to concentrate on her aunt's behavior. That way she could remain detached and aloof for the next few days. Indeed, why her aunt felt the need to get rid of her was a puzzlement. What sort of threat did she present to her that necessitated such a drastic step? Jealousy surely could not be the only motivation, unless it was tinged with a terrible madness.

Someone jostled her rudely and awoke her from her reverie. "Why don't yer watch where's yer going, miss?" a man snarled. "The pavement's for the use of all us folks, not just you."

"I . . . I am so sorry . . ." Felicia began but realized that she was speaking to herself, the rude man having disappeared into the crowd.

Oh! dear, she thought guiltily as she became aware of the advanced hour, Lady Louisa will be worried if I don't return soon. She looked around for a hansom as the ones for hire usually stood at street corners. But to her dismay, she realized that she had wandered into an unknown part of London. There was nothing familiar at all, either in her immediate surroundings or in the higher buildings beyond. Her face wore a worried frown as she looked round for a kindly face in the throng to whom she could turn for directions to Berkeley Square. As she did so, her eyes were drawn to an open barouche that was approaching at a steady pace. With a fascinated horror, Felicia found herself looking at her aunt, who was sitting regally in one corner. Momentarily paralyzed, Felicia watched as the carriage drew nearer, and it was only when she realized that her aunt had seen her that she attempted to move away and seek shelter in a near-by doorway.

She turned swiftly and started to run just as she heard a voice command, "Stop that thief! That young girl, there. She tried to snatch my reticule."

Felicia did not stop in the ensuing confusion, seizing the opportunity to get away, although the loud voice followed her.

"That girl, there. The one in the gray dress. Quick, you imbecile, before she gets away."

Suddenly Felicia felt a hand on her shoulder, and she was spun around.

"This be the one, ma'am?" an elderly man shouted above the crowd as Felicia struggled under the firm grasp. "Oh! No, you don't, you young bit of vermin, you. Don't think of trying to get away, because I've got you good and tight." As if to prove his point, he gripped her right arm and twisted it behind her back.

"Please, sir," Felicia whispered, as a pain ripped through her body. "Please let me go. There has been an awful mistake."

"You explain that to the policeman, then, and see what 'e 'as to say. But I doubt 'e'll take your word for it against the lady what 'as made the charge. It's for people like you that we 'ave the Penal Colony—'anging's too good for the likes of you."

The crowd murmured its approval of these sentiments, and Felicia cut short her protests as she felt their hostility. In the meantime, Lady Ormstead, descending from her carriage, had made her way through the throng to Felicia.

"Yes, my good man. That's the girl that tried to steal my reticule. And, but for you she would have succeeded in getting away." She pressed a coin in the man's free hand, and for the benefit of the crowd shuddered in distaste as she looked at Felicia.

"I think you have made a grave mistake, ma'am." Felicia repeated, unable to stay the tremor in her voice. She turned to the crowd again. "If someone would be so kind as to . . . as to . . ." she broke off lamely, realizing that she simply could not invoke Lord Umber's name in front of all those people. Far better to wait for the policeman as it would undoubtedly be easier to explain to him the awful predicament she now found herself in.

She stiffened as she felt, rather than saw, the look of loathing her aunt bestowed on her and quickly turned to look at her. "Why are you doing this to me, ma'am? What have I or my parents done to you to warrant such treatment?" Although her voice was calm now, Felicia could not control her trembling. Viciously, the man twisted her arm back even further, causing her to cry out in pain.

" 'Ere, 'ave a 'eart," a woman in the crowd shouted out, "you don't 'ave to be so bloody brutal."

"Watch yer language in front of the lady," a fat man rejoined, pointing to Lady Ormstead. "We don't want to frighten 'er off." With an ugly laugh he wiped a greasy hand across his unshaven face.

Lady Ormstead looked disdainfully at the man before turning to Felicia. "It will be as well for you, to keep your questions to yourself," she sneered. "I have nothing to say to the likes of you."

"But, Aunt . . ." Felicia began.

"That's enough. You 'eard what the lady said. She ain't got nothing to say to you."

Before Felicia could continue, the crowd separated as two policemen approached, bent on investigating the cause of the disturbance. Swinging their truncheons, they surveyed the crowd, poking a few slow movers out of their way.

"'Ello, 'ello. What 'ave we 'ere then?" the older one said.

"It's the young vermin, officer," several voices chanted. "She tried to snatch the lady's bag."

The policeman turned to Lady Ormstead. "Is that the truth, ma'am?" Lady Ormstead nodded. "Well, we'll soon 'ave 'er under lock and key. We can't 'ave gentry 'armed like that."

Felicia cast an appealing look to the stolid figure who had spoken, but before she could utter a word, Lady Ormstead stepped forward. "Indeed, officer, I agree with your sentiments. It is as these good people say. This . . .

this . . . person attempted to steal my reticule, and the very kind gentleman there managed to apprehend her as she ran away." She opened her purse and pulled out a card. "Here is my direction. I will be glad to answer any questions you may have, at my convenience. Now, if it is all right, I would like to proceed."

The policeman nodded, dumbstruck by the authority with which she spoke, and quite overawed by her grand manner. "Of . . . of . . . course, your Ladyship," he stuttered, pocketing the card without looking at it, as he recognized the feel of a coin sandwiched between his hand and the card.

He stepped up to Felicia and, rising to the importance of the occasion, intoned, "You 'ave 'eard the charges that will be brought against you, so you best come with me without any more fuss." None too gently he freed Felicia from the elderly man's grip and ordered a path be made for them. "Anyone what witnessed the criminal act line up 'ere and give the necessary information to my friend." He passed on, pulling Felicia behind him.

Furious with herself for getting into such a predicament, Felicia allowed herself to be led away, for one look at the set features of her new captor convinced her that he was too full of himself to listen to her story in front of so many people. And, more importantly, she did not want to give anyone, especially her aunt, the satisfaction of seeing her beg for mercy. So, with her head thrust proudly in the air, she walked away, gracefully sidestepping the various obstacles that the crowd spitefully put in her way.

Once out of earshot, Felicia turned to the policeman

and in her well-modulated voice begged that he listen to her story.

Reluctantly he slowed his pace and took a closer look at his charge. He was surprised to find that he was looking at a young girl, who, although visibly nervous, appeared dignified and well-dressed.

"Please, please, you must listen to me. It really is a terrible mistake. That woman who accused me of trying to steal her reticule is my aunt. . . ."

"Yes, yes," the policeman said resignedly. "And she is trying to get rid of you in order to get 'er 'ands on your fortune. You'll 'ave to do better than that, my girl."

"It is true that she is trying to get rid of me," Felicia protested. "But certainly not because of any fortune. Please say you will help me." She paused, wondering what inducement she could offer to sway him.

"Now why should I take your word against that of such a fine lady?" He felt in his pocket as he spoke for the coin. "Don't think you're the first one with the story of the wicked aunt, 'cause you isn't."

"But you must believe me," Felicia pleaded, a note of desperation creeping into her voice. "This time it is the truth. Please, officer."

There was a genuine note of suffering in her voice which caught the policeman's ear. "I dunno 'as 'ow I can, miss. See, it's against the regulations once I 'ave you in my custody, to do anything more than take you to Newgate." He scratched his head as he pondered his problem. "No. The only thing for me to do is to take you there and let justice take its proper course."

"Not Newgate," Felicia cried out, a look of horrified

revulsion spreading across her face. "You cannot mean it, sir. Why . . . why . . . that is a place for criminals."

"Still acting the innocent, are we?" the policeman snapped, his patience wearing thin. "Well, what do you think you is then? You're a bleeding criminal, and I'm taking you where you belong."

For the second time time that morning, Felicia felt blackness enveloping her, and the policeman caught her as she sagged against him limply.

Pity for her stirred him again, for she did look like a decent young woman. He wondered why she had turned to purse-snatching and then shrugged his shoulders carelessly. He mustn't get too soft, he thought, just because she reminded him a little of his own daughter. He looked round, trying to locate the police wagon and finally saw it further down the street. Catching the eye of the driver, he beckoned him nearer and without further ado picked Felicia up and tossed her into the back of the wagon, shutting and bolting the doors with a bang.

"You can explain all that to Mistress James, and see if she'll 'elp you," he called to Felicia as he swung himself up beside the driver. "And see if she believes your story of a wicked aunt." He turned to the driver and grinned conspiratorily. "Wicked aunt, indeed. It's always a wonder the lies these sluts will think up next."

"She don't look like no common slut to me," the driver answered, drawing his top lip over his blackened front teeth in a semblance of a grin. "More like some fine lord 'as tossed 'er out after he 'ad 'is fill."

"Well, that's 'er problem, air't it now. We'll just 'ave to wait and see if anyone comes to claim 'er."

Once inside the high stone walls of the prison, Felicia

came to. Fearfully, she tried to comprehend where she was and what had happened, when the policeman dragged her from the wagon into the pale light that was filtering through the clouds, casting a gloomy lambency in the yard. The name David Burton flashed through her mind. Why hadn't she thought of him sooner? He was certain to help. Comforted by her thoughts, Felicia looked at her jailor with more courage.

"Whom do I see now?" she asked. "I wish to inform my solicitor of this unfortunate mistake immediately."

"Oh! We do 'ave our airs and graces, don't we? Solicitor, is it now? Well, you just wait until Mistress James 'as seen you and sees if you still want to see your legal man then."

Something in his sneer caused Felicia's newfound courage to evaporate, but with a determination born of fear she ignored his remark. "How much do you want?" she asked with a sudden foresight, "to put me in a private room so that I can write to my friend *before* I see this Mistress James?"

The policeman eyed her greedily. It wouldn't harm anyone, he thought, if he took her to the smaller office building for a while. "What 'ave you got?"

Reluctantly Felicia opened her purse and exposed the few coins she had. "That is all I have until Mr. Burton arrives," she answered. "But I know he will reward you handsomely for the inconvenience I have caused you."

"Mr. Burton, you say?" the policeman asked sharply, as he quickly pocketed the money. "You 'ave some mighty powerful friends, don't you?"

Felicia smiled grimly at the sudden change in his attitude and pressed her advantage. "Mr. Burton is a good family friend and would not like it if I tell him how I have been ill-treated. . . ."

"You just follow me, now, miss, and I'll see that you is made comfortable," the policeman said quickly. "Mr. Burton is well-known around 'ere for 'is influence. So you just tell 'im that Jack Walsh looked after you."

Relieved that her ploy had worked, Felicia was thankful when they reached a small, stuffy backroom. "If you would be so kind as to fetch me a quill and some paper, I can notify Mr. Burton of my situation. And, if possible, I would like a candle."

The policeman left her, carefully locking the door behind him. "No use in taking chances," he muttered to himself. "Just because she said she knows Mr. Burton don't mean that she'll get any 'elp from him. And that lady what wants to press charges, she looks to be a mean character that would cause trouble if she could. Go carefully, Jack, me boy. Go carefully."

Left alone, Felicia took in her surroundings at one glance. Thick dust formed a layer over everything, and a sudden movement in one corner of the wainscot indicated the presence of a rat. Thankful that her years of country living had innured her to that particular rodent, she ignored the noise and set about cleaning off the table that stood in the middle of the room. Any activity was better than just standing still. Having done the best she could with her thin linen handkerchief, she crossed to the heavily barred window and stared out at the cobblestone yard miserably. Once again she tried to organize her thoughts. She deliberately ignored the images of Lord Umber that kept forcing their way into her mind and concentrated instead on what she ought to say to David. Obviously, she couldn't tell him everything, and pride would prohibit her from mentioning the part her aunt had played in her arrest. She must be concise yet clear.

The scraping of the key in the lock brought her attention back to her surroundings.

"I did the best I could, miss," Jack Walsh said defensively as he laid the items she had requested on the table. "But candles are difficult to come by 'ere."

"It is adequate," Felicia said, hurrying over, eyeing the small stub of wax that would have to do as a temporary light. "Thank you. It won't take me long to draft my note." She bent over the table and started to write. Within minutes she had filled the sheet of paper and folding it in two, wrote David's office address on the one flap. "Mr. Burton's offices are at 40 Lincoln's Inn, Mr. Walsh, and I am certain that his senior clerk will give you an extra guinea for delivering this." She felt it necessary to dangle the enticement of further monetary rewards in front of him, for she was beginning to realize that it was the only language he understood. "Before you go, perhaps you could tell me how you know of Mr. Burton. I did not realize his reputation extended this far."

" 'Im is well-known around 'ere, because 'e goes out of 'is way to defend the lowest of the low. 'Im and the judge, Lord Davenport, work together. If the judge is presiding, like, then you can be certain that Mr. Burton is defending. It's a funny sort of justice they dole out, but they treat everyone fair. Unlike some I could mention."

"I see," Felicia responded, not understanding. David seemed far too young to have gained such fame for himself . . . and quite what sort of justice he and this judge meted out was beyond her comprehension.

"And if you say 'e's a friend of the family, then maybe you knows all about 'ow 'e and some lord look after the children of convicted felons."

"Not very much," Felicia said hastily, wondering if this was the charity Lord Umber was involved in. "Mr. Burton is very modest and does not talk too much of his good works."

Jack Walsh smacked his lips together as an idea formed in his mind. "See, if you really knows this Mr. Burton and you was to draw my name to 'is attention, then it's possible, if you say the right thing so to speak, that 'e would consider putting me and my missus in charge of one of these 'omes he 'as for the urchins."

"The kindness you have shown me, Mr. Walsh, is certainly something to commend," Felicia said diplomatically, trying at the same time to still the warm feeling that her captor's words had evoked. For some inexplicable reason she knew that the lord he referred to was Lord Umber, and the elation she felt was caused by the knowledge that he was as generous to the underprivileged as he was kind to his mother. How she had misjudged him! "And . . . and . . . you may rest assured that I will certainly mention your name to Mr. Burton."

He regarded her shrewdly for a moment. "Well, I'll be on my way, then, miss, else I'll not get back afore nightfall."

"Perhaps you could tell me one other thing before you go, Mr. Walsh. The crime I am supposed to have committed, what . . . what is the penalty?"

"Death by 'anging, miss, or deportation. Depending, of course, on the evidence," he added quickly as he saw the color drain from Felicia's face. "It's a serious crime, miss, no matter who you are."

"But I am innocent," Felicia whispered. "Innocent. Please hurry with my note. I shall only rest easy when I know that it has been safely delivered."

"You rely on Jack Walsh, miss. I'll see to it that Mr. Burton gets this. And if it makes you feel better, I'll make arrangements for you to be locked in this 'ere room until I return. It'll cost a bit more than you 'ave given me, but I reckon we can settle the score when Mr. Burton gets 'ere."

"But what of this Mistress James you spoke of? Will she not be expecting me?"

"Don't you be worrying your pretty head over 'er. There being no rush to move you immediately, especially when I say the word."

"Well, thank you, Mr. Walsh," Felicia said forlornly. "I really don't know what I would have done without you."

"Easy on, miss," he said in alarm. "Don't go fainting away again on me. Nobody's going to harm you yet. And, what's more, if you really do know Mr. Burton, maybe 'e can even get the lady to drop all charges. 'E can be very persuasive, I'm told. Anyways, I'm doing no more for you than I would 'ope anyone would do for my daughter if, Lord 'elp us, she were ever to find herself in similar circumstances."

Felicia smiled at him wanly, knowing that his only motivation was greed. But she was too thankful that he had agreed to help her to care. "I shall wait for you to return then."

Thirteen

There was such a smug, well-satisfied air about Lady Ormstead when she returned to her rented house in Upper Grosvenor Street that the footman commented on it to Mr. Nestor. " 'Erself is a delight this noon, and 'ere's me be'en worrying that she would be letting me go for my failure to give the gentleman the message this morning. Wonders will never cease, will they, Mr. Nestor?"

The butler gave him a frosty look before replying. "If it's Lady Ormstead you is referring to, then kindly say so, lad. I don't know really what the agency was a-thinking of, sending you 'ere as an experienced footman. I, myself, 'ave never encountered such unfamiliarity as to 'ow to comport oneself about one's duties as you display." He sniffed haughtily in what he considered his most superior manner, but the footman seemed quite unabashed.

"Aw, come off it, Mr. Nestor. You know the agency 'ad no one else to send 'ere. It must be seven poor souls like me that 'erself, begging your pardon, Lady Ormstead, has gobbled up this Season, and I only undertook the position to get experience. For I am going to be a gentleman's gentleman one day." He grinned impishly at the impassive face of his mentor.

"Then you 'ad better learn 'ow to behave in the presence of one," Mr. Nestor answered scathingly, "and make sure that you deliver the correct message to that Lord Umber when 'e calls again." His homily was interrupted by the sound of Lady Ormstead's bell, and without more ado he moved away to answer the summons.

"You rang, my lady?" he inquired grandly when he finally reached Lady Ormstead's sitting room.

"Yes, Nestor. I have changed my mind about not seeing Lord Umber this afternoon. So when he calls kindly see to it that he is shown into the brown room."

"If you don't mind me mentioning it, your Ladyship, the fire smokes something terrible in that room. Perhaps I could suggest the library." He coughed deprecatingly.

"No. No, Nestor. Just do as I tell you. He won't stay long enough to worry about a few plumes of smoke." Her eyes glistened with suppressed excitement. "And there is no need for you to stay in the vicinity."

"I beg your pardon, madam?"

"Eavesdropping, Nestor, eavesdropping."

"Madam!" the butler exclaimed in outraged tones. "I 'ave never been guilty of such an atrocious act in all my life."

"Good, good," Lady Ormstead said unpleasantly. "Just insure you don't change your habits today."

"Is that all, then, madam?" he inquired stiffly, checking his anger with difficulty at her vulgarity. All his sensibilities were offended by her suggestion.

Lady Ormstead dismissed him with a wave and an order to send Wendy to her, before sitting back to contemplate the upcoming interview. "I do believe I have done it," she said to herself gleefully. "This time, I think I have succeeded, and now no one need ever know that Richard and Arabella had a daughter." She let out a mad cackle which shook her voluminous body like a partly set jelly.

"Mama, Mama, are you all right?"

The anxious voice of her daughter brought Lady Ormstead out of her daydream abruptly. "What is it, child?" she asked sharply. "How many times do I have to tell you not to creep up on me? You know any sudden movement is bad for my heart. Really, Wendy, you are so thoughtless."

Wendy stood to one side, biting nervously on her lower lip. "I'm sorry, Mama," she whined. "But Nestor said you wanted to see me."

Lady Ormstead eyed her daughter keenly before turning her gaze in the direction of the window. It really was too provoking that she had been blessed with such an obese daughter. Absolutely nothing could be done to disguise those pimples which covered her face. As for the child's figure, no amount of lacing would produce the small waistline that was so fashionable. And to crown it all, they had not received a single invitation that amounted to anything. The outrage of seeing Felicia, whom she had thought to be out of sight for ever, perched happily between Lord Umber and his dowager mother, was too much to bear with comfort. Why, Wendy had not met a single eligible male, and the only offer had come from their neighbor, Mr. Brown, who was old enough to be a grandfather. She muttered under her breath savagely. "It would serve her right if I accept."

"I beg your pardon, Mama? I . . . I didn't hear."

"Don't interrupt, Wendy. Do sit down and stop fidgeting, and smooth your dress, you look an absolute fright."

"Yes, Mama. I'm sorry, Mama," Wendy whined as she obeyed.

"I want you to know that you have received your first offer, and I am at this very moment considering whether to accept it."

"Yes, Mama," Wendy said dully.

"Do you not want to know who has honored you so? Really, you are an exasperating child. Nothing, it seems, interests you except cream buns and bon bons. Mr. Brown is most anxious to take you off my hands."

"Mr. Brown, Mama!" Wendy exclaimed in agitation. "How . . . how could he? He doesn't even know me except to say 'good morning.' Why, I have never given him the slightest encouragement. Please, Mama, I couldn't possibly. He's . . . he's . . . far too old, and besides, he's deaf."

"I haven't given him my answer yet, Wendy, so don't be in such a taking. Although the way you behave at the dances I take you to does not lend much encouragement to any of the younger men. You are a wallflower, my dear," she said spitefully, "and a wilting one at that."

"But, Mama," Wendy snivelled. "It's not my fault. If only you could find me a maid like Felicia. I know I would look better, but . . . but, the one we have now is worse than Sadie. No one is able to dress my hair like Felicia. No one. Why did you have to send her away.?"

"Who?" Lady Ormstead said in a dangerously quiet voice. "Whom are you talking about? Have I not forbidden you ever to mention that name in my presence? Have I not ordered you to forget that she ever existed? I will not be disobeyed, Wendy. Now, go to your room and remain there for the rest of the day. And, if you continue to disregard my wishes, I will accept Mr. Brown's offer and let him drum some sense into you."

A storm of tears shook Wendy, and soon she was sobbing hysterically. "Please, Mama," she begged. "Please don't do that. And I am sorry to have disobeyed you. I promise it won't happen again. Only, please, please don't say yes to Mr. Brown."

"Go to your room immediately," Lady Ormstead said irritably. "I have had enough of your tantrums. Spend the rest of the day comtemplating the trouble you have caused me, and maybe by tomorrow I will feel more inclined to forgive you."

Wendy fled, crying uncontrollably, leaving her mother looking at the closed door with a pleased expression on her face. Now, she could rest easy, for her interview with Lord Umber would not be interrupted. She knew that Wendy would not dare to come downstairs for the rest of the day.

The peace and quiet of White's had done much to restore Lord Umber's humor, and he had just finished reading the morning papers when he felt someone tapping his shoulder. He looked round and saw, to his surprise, that Dr. Ross was standing behind him. Rising quickly, he followed him out of the reading room.

"Paul, my dear fellow, to what do I owe this honor? I have never seen you out of your place before late afternoon."

Dr. Ross smiled. "I was hoping you would invite me to join you for a spot of lunch. And I do leave my offices, you know, on occasion."

"Luncheon? What a splendid idea. Excuse me while I organize a table." He clicked his fingers at a passing waiter and said something quietly. He nodded at the reply and turned back to Dr. Ross. "Follow me, Paul. It appears we can be accommodated immediately."

Neither man spoke as they were ushered into the high-domed dining room and led to a solitary table in the far corner. Only after they had ordered did Dr. Ross break the companionable silence.

"Ian, I know it is presumptuous of me, but I beg your understanding and indulgence."

"Whatever for, Paul. Surely we have known each other too long to be so formal. Whatever is bothering you so?"

Dr. Ross hesitated for a moment. "I . . . I want to talk to you about Miss Richards."

"Aha! Your favorite patient. Why the serious air?" Even though he tried to be casual, a note of resignation crept into his voice. It seemed everyone was conspiring to make it more difficult than he had anticipated to forget about Felicia.

"We had, at least from my point of view, a very good session this morning, in that Miss Richards remembered everything. She knows who she is, who her parents were and, more importantly, who Lady Ormstead is." Dr. Ross sat back in his chair, wondering what it was that had prompted him to interfere and which was the best way to proceed now. The withdrawn expression on Lord Umber's face indicated that his friend might well be relieved by Felicia's decision to leave Lady Louisa's household. "The result is that she has decided to seek gainful employment elsewhere."

"I see," Lord Umber said thoughtfully, wondering why this information displeased him. "She is quite determined this time, I suppose?"

Dr. Ross nodded. "My concern, of course, is for your mother, but Miss Richards feels that she cannot accept her charity indefinitely, even though she has grown extremely fond of Lady Louisa. . . ."

"What prompted this decision, Paul?" Lord Umber broke in impatiently. "Something that happened in her past that makes her an unfit companion? Was I right, all along, about her true profession?" He suppressed a bitterness he suddenly felt with difficulty.

"No, indeed not, Ian. As far as I know she has impeccable credentials. But you must have observed how independent she is. It is this spirit of independence that is prompting her to make her own way in the world. In fact, the only reason I mention any of this is that I want your assurances you will not make her leaving any more difficult than it is going to be."

There was a hidden meaning to the words that Lord Umber was astute enough to recognize, but not clairvoyant enough to understand. His only reaction was to raise an eyebrow as though in query. "Whatever do you mean by that, Paul? I can hardly chain her to my mother's side, can I? If Miss Richards is really of a mind to leave, then I shall do my utmost to aid her. And by that, I mean I shall insure mama does not go to any great lengths to prevent Miss Richards from doing as she wants." As he was speaking, his one hand was unconsciously stroking his cravat, which was the only sign Dr. Ross's trained eye that something was bothering him. But Dr. Ross was wise enough to know that he would have to content himself with these assurances. It would serve no useful purpose to probe Lord Umber's feelings on the subject. "Good. Then I can put my concern aside for both my patients and do justice to this meal."

Lord Umber watched his friend for a few moments while he struggled to appear calm. His earlier resolution of getting on with his own life suddenly seemed hollow as the knowledge that he would never see Felicia again penetrated. What nonsense had gotten into her that made her so independent? For someone as intelligent as he knew her to be, she was quite senseless at times.

"As a matter of curiosity, Paul, who is Lady Ormstead? I called on her this morning but was refused admittance."

Dr. Ross wavered for a second before answering. "Lady Ormstead is an aunt of Miss Richards, I believe. They are not very close."

Lord Umber thought back to last night at the theater. "Judging from her behavior towards Miss Richards last night, I am inclined to believe you." Again he appeared casual, but his senses were alert. Something was not quite right about the story that Dr. Ross was telling him. "I had intended calling on her again, but if you say that Miss Richards' memory has returned, then I will gladly forfeit that dubious pleasure. Do you agree?"

"Absolutely, Ian. Another attempt seems quite unnecessary now. Also, I am sure Miss Richards would prefer that you didn't."

The response was too quick, but Lord Umber let it go. There seemed little point in pursuing something his friend quite obviously did not want to discuss. "If you say so, Paul," he said smoothly, while vowing to himself to keep the appointment. Was there indeed something in Miss Richards' background that needed burying? "What of this trip to Manchester, Paul? What explanation did Miss Richards have for that?"

"A fairly simple one, actually. She had the wrong address. When I confronted her with that, she was not at all perturbed, for it appears she has relatives there and would not have experienced any difficulty. Certainly none of the nature Lady Louisa envisaged," Dr. Ross lied and was astonished that he should have done so. But as Ian seemed satisfied with his explanation, he felt well justified. All he had to remember now was to tell Felicia not to contradict his story.

"So all our concern was for naught, eh? What a bunch of worry warts we have been." He raised his wine goblet in a toast. "Here's to you, Paul, and for the remarkable success you have achieved. May Anton Mesmer be equally delighted."

"Thank you, Ian. Thank you. I must confess to a great feeling of elation, for there were many times when I doubted my ability to break through that barrier. There were two main clues that helped. . . ."

Lord Umber sat still, giving every outward appearance that his full attention was with his friend. In truth, though, he was thinking of Felicia and the extraordinary behavior of Dr. Ross. There was something highly suspicious about the whole affair. Not that he doubted the part about Felicia's memory returning. It was just a feeling he had, but nothing he could put his finger on. However, there was no denying the fact that Paul was bent on protecting her. What from, he could not fathom. But surely that was his prerogative. Surprised at the intensity of his feelings, he tried to channel his thoughts away from Felicia. Impatiently he took out his fob watch and saw that it lacked but forty minutes to three. "I hate to interrupt your dissertation, Paul," he said hastily, "but I have a previous engagement. Please excuse me."

"My dear Ian, I have been finished these last five minutes," Dr. Ross laughed. "We have been sitting in silence ever since."

Lord Umber had the grace to look sheepish. "Do excuse my apparent rudeness, it was not intended. I . . . I was planning a diversion for my mother to help her over Miss Richards' departure."

"I understand," Dr. Ross said gently. "And please call on me if I can help." He stood up and strolled out of the room, waving casually to a few acquaintances.

Lord Umber followed and, calling for his carriage, was soon on his way to Upper Grosvenor Street.

It was quite apparent that his second visit to Lady Ormstead's was going to be more successful. For no sooner had his carriage come to rest outside the house, than the front door swung open and an immaculately dressed footman made his appearance. Lord Umber was hard put to recognize the lackey from his earlier visit, such was the change in that poor unfortunate's countenance.

"I see I am expected," he drawled, deliberately stating

the obvious. He tossed his hat and gloves into the out-stretched hands.

Mr. Nestor stepped forward from a darkened recess, lending a surprisingly dignified atmosphere to the shabby interior, before any further exchange could take place. "This way, your lordship," he intoned heavily. "Lady Ormstead will be with you momentarily."

Concealing his distaste at the drab room he was shown to, Lord Umber walked over to the smoking fire and idly kicked at the sullen embers. The door, badly in need of an oiling, creaked to a close behind the butler, and he was left alone. "In many ways it is my own fault," he mused. "If I had heeded Paul's advice, I would be in much more comfortable surroundings." He looked around the room with disdain. The cheap furnishings, the threadbare carpet, and the peeling paint denoted 'genteel' poverty and probably indicated that Lady Ormstead clung to the fringes of Society by a hair's-breadth. *She might be more successful if she were more pleasant,* he thought savagely. He crossed to the windows and stared out at a row of red brick houses, grimacing at the view. It was difficult to imagine Felicia in these surroundings. Tantamount to caging an exotic bird. But if what Paul had said was true, she was not very close to this aunt. However, he thought triumphantly, that did not mean she had not made her home here, for had not David said he remembered a Mrs. Richards had been in attendance when he had visited Lady Ormstead? He frowned at this recollection, wondering again why Paul had been so evasive at lunch. Protecting his patient's confidence, no doubt. Nonetheless, it was provoking, and he should have guessed sooner that Felicia was behind it. Now why should she want her past kept a secret? What shameful act had she committed? He felt a momentary pleasure as he imagined the worst before rejecting the thought. No, she was incapable of doing anything so monumentally distasteful, he assured himself. The reason she wanted to seek employment elsewhere must have been caused by something her parents had done.

Her image flashed in front of him and he felt an odd choking sensation constrict his heart. Confound the girl, would he ever forget her?

His musings were rudely interrupted at that point, as the creaking door announced the arrival of Lady Ormstead. She bustled into the room, smiling grandly. "I do beg your pardon, Lord Umber, for keeping you waiting. Pray be seated." She indicated a most uncomfortable-looking chair right beside the smoking fire, while she herself took what had to be the only commodious seat in the room.

Lord Umber glanced at the clock on the mantelshelf and saw with surprise that he had been kept waiting fifteen minutes. He turned a bored look on his hostess. "Thank you, but no. I do not intend making this a long visit." He arched one eyebrow as he spoke, unconsciously presenting a formidable appearance. "I merely came to enquire about Miss Richards. Your niece, I believe?"

Lady Ormstead stared at him in fascination. His immaculate dress gave him an indefinable air that was almost intimidating. It was only her secret knowledge of Felicia's whereabouts that bolstered her spirit. "What has my niece been doing now, pray? Not, I hope, causing more embarrassment for my family." There was a long-suffering edge to her voice, as though she were trying to convey to her audience how ill-used she had been.

"Your niece, ma'am, was injured in an accident which caused the loss of her memory for a short period."

"How inconvenient," Lady Ormstead murmured unsympathetically. "She is recovered, I take it?"

Lord Umber noted the nervous way this question was asked and replied grimly. "Totally. You do not seem overly concerned that your niece was injured."

"And I do not see that that is any concern of yours," Lady Ormstead snapped, wondering how this gentleman had met Felicia and just what he knew. Far better to attack than defend, she thought as she continued briskly. "I will say one thing, though, and that is her ingratitude at the hospitality I showed her—and her mother—seems to have been well rewarded. I have not seen her since she ran away several weeks ago."

"Until last night," Lord Umber reminded her.

"Or someone who bore a resemblance, my lord. One thing I know for a certainty, my niece never owned such finery as that girl wore. And if that was she, it can only mean that she did not come by it honestly."

Lord Umber looked away in disgust at the implication of her words but did not yield to the temptation of telling her the truth.

"One thing you may be sure of, Lord Umber," Lady Ormstead continued maliciously, "I will never recognize her again. And should she try and worm her way back into my household, I will personally see to it that she is put back out on the streets—for that is where she belongs. And why a fine young gentleman like yourself should be bothering about such a good-for-nothing girl as Felicia, I'll never know."

The raw-edged bitterness of her voice puzzled Lord Umber. He had not said anything to provoke such an outburst, and yet this crazed woman had made it quite clear that she regarded Felicia as little more than a slut. " 'Tis no more than a kindness I would show any stray animal," he replied suavely. "However, I shall not take up any more of your time, for the purpose of my visit was to enquire about Miss Richards' relatives and possibly restore her to them."

A relieved look tinged Lady Ormstead's plump features as the realization came to her that Felicia had not spoken of the five years spent at Graystones. She suppressed a satisfied grin with difficulty. "I'll bid you good day then, my lord. I am sorry your journey has been for naught, but I do not expect that Felicia will ever come here again, begging for help. Especially after what she did before she ran off."

Malicious as well as stupid, Lord Umber thought disdainfully. Does she not realize that her disinterest in the whereabouts of Felicia strikes me as suspicious? That her determination to smear Felicia's name makes me mistrust her even more. He drew himself up to his full height, looking down on her with contempt. "I will personally insure that Miss Richards does not bother you again, for it is quite obvious that she is better off where she is." So saying, he took out a delicate, blue enamel snuff box from his vest pocket and opened it expertly with one hand. He took a small pinch and inhaled it deeply. His gaze, however, did not waver from Lady Ormstead's face so he did not miss the exultant look that lit her eyes. Now, what the devil can have caused that? he asked himself uneasily. She was altogether too complacent. Had Felicia already been to see her to ask for help?

Impatiently he started for the door, for he wanted to check for himself that Felicia was safely at home with his mother. "I will see myself out, ma'am. Good day." He snapped the noisy door shut behind him and waited while the footman fetched his hat and gloves. Impulsively, he pulled a coin out of his pocket and pressed it into the lackey's hand. "Has a Miss Richards visited with Lady Ormstead today?" he asked casually.

"No . . . no . . . me lord. You're the only bit of gentry that 'as called."

"Do you know if Miss Richards has ever been here?" he pressed.

"No . . . not that I can recall," the footman answered, wrinkling up his nose in concentration. "No. That name is not one I've 'eard afore."

"I see. Thank you." Lord Umber stepped out of the house with a sigh of relief and ordered his coachman to spring the horses to his mother's house. He felt something was wrong and needed to seek reassurance that Felicia was well.

After his departure, Lady Ormstead sat for several minutes laughing to herself. "Oh! yes, my fine young dandy. Felicia is far better off where she is. Far better off. And don't think you can come back again and bamboozle me into telling you anything more. Ha! Ha! No one is ever going to find you now, Felicia. No one." She stood up abruptly and rang the bell several times.

After what seemed to her an interminable wait, Mr. Nestor appeared. "You rang, your ladyship?"

"Several times, Nestor." She paced the room as she spoke. "I want you to insure that Lord Umber is never admitted again, if he should call. Is that clear?"

"Perfectly, your ladyship."

"Good. I will hold you responsible if my order is disobeyed. I shall be in my sitting room if Mr. Brown calls. Kindly show him there when he arrives." Without waiting for an answer she left the room, leaving in her wake an echo of triumphant laughter.

Fourteen

Lord Umber and David arrived at Lady Louisa's house together, and the air of suppressed excitement that enveloped David did much to dissipate the feeling of foreboding Lord Umber had.

"Ian," David exclaimed happily, "the very person I would want to be present when I tell Miss Richards who she is."

"She already knows, David," Lord Umber replied, his voice heavy with disappointment. "Her memory returned this morning."

"Ah! but I have information that even she knows nothing of. Come, let us go inside and give her the good news."

Once again Lord Umber's spirits rose, for David's good humor was infectious. However, the atmosphere in the house was oppressive, and both men looked at each other in alarm. The unusually somber face of Sims, the butler, indicated that something was amiss and the way the footman refused to raise his eyes from the intricate mosaic pattern of the tiled floor confirmed this.

"Is everything all right, Sims?" Lord Umber inquired.

The butler indicated the blue saloon with some distress. "Lady Louisa is anxious to see you, your lordship. I . . . I . . ."

"Well, what is it, Sims? For God's sake, tell me what has happened."

"It's Miss Richards, your lordship. It appears that she has disappeared."

David looked at Lord Umber quickly and saw the naked despair that clouded his friend's eyes. *Egad!* he thought, *Ian really is in love with the chit. I wonder if he knows it.*

"Thank you, Sims," Lord Umber said heavily. "No, no, there is no need to announce us. Let us see what all this is about, David." He moved forward, and David followed him tentatively.

"There must be an explanation, Ian," he said gently. "Mayhap she went to exchange a book at the library, or even lost herself for an hour or two in the Pantheon."

"Of course, David. There is bound to be a simple answer. It is just that I spent a rather unpleasant afternoon with Miss Richards' aunt, Lady Ormstead, and now this news. Frankly, it makes me feel uneasy. I fear Lady Ormstead is quite mad and has something to do with Miss Richards' nonappearance."

"Lady Ormstead said something that indicated her involvement?" David asked.

"Ever the solicitor, David, aren't you? No, she said nothing—it was all in her attitude." He opened the door softly. "Let us do what we can to reassure Mama that all is well."

The sight that greeted them was far from reassuring. Lady Louisa was prone on a pretty chintz chaise, and Dr. Ross was standing over her feeling her pulse. He turned around at the sound of voices and smiled encouragingly. "It is not as bad as it looks, Ian," he comforted, carefully placing Lady Louisa's arm across her chest. "I have just given her a dose of laudanum to ease her anxiety, otherwise she is perfectly well." He moved over to his friends as he spoke. "Is there another room we can use? I think it as well for Lady Louisa to rest for a while."

"The study," Lord Umber said quickly. "This way." He led the party out into the hallway and pointed to a door diagonally opposite. "In there. I will join you in a moment." He beckoned the footman over who had been hovering nearby and ordered some refreshments.

"Yes, m'lord. Right away, sir," he said with respect and scurried off to do as he was bade.

As Lord Umber entered the library, he cast an apprehensive look at Dr. Ross. "I take it the disappearance of Miss Richards caused Mama to react as she did? Nothing more serious?"

"That's about it, Ian. She has spent most of the morning until now," he pulled out his fob watch, "that's almost five hours, working herself into this state. When Miss Richards failed to return from her appointment with me by noon, Lady Louisa sent a servant to my office. Unfortunately I had already left for my luncheon with you, and instead of returning to Lady Louisa, the silly man decided he'd best stay put until I came back."

"What time did you return?" David asked.

"Not more than fifty minutes ago." He turned to Lord Umber apologetically. "I met some colleagues on my way out of White's, otherwise I would have returned much earlier."

"Ian tells me that Miss Richards' memory returned completely, Paul. Would this occurrence have caused her to run away?"

"No. Not at all. She made up her mind to seek employment elsewhere, but had agreed to stay with Lady Louisa until another position could be found."

David looked at Dr. Ross quizzically, but Lord Umber intercepted the question. "It would appear she did not want to become a charitable case," he said. "Are you positive, Paul, that she was perfectly composed when she left you? There's no chance she could have undergone a change of mind because of something she had recalled that was shaming?"

"You have my word, Ian, that Miss Richards had no reason to be ashamed of anything. Her father was killed in a duel nearly six years ago, whereupon her mother was forced to seek Lady Ormstead's aid. They made their home with her until Mrs. Richards died. It was then that Felicia . . . I mean Miss Richards . . . left to go to Manchester."

"It all seems unexceptionable to me," David said at length, quite forgetting the news he had to impart as his mind tried to unravel the mystery. "Perhaps Miss Richards has returned to Lady Ormstead."

"No," Lord Umber said flatly. "As I mentioned to you,

I have just returned from visiting that woman," he turned to Dr. Ross and smiled briefly. "I couldn't resist the temptation."

Dr. Ross smiled in understanding.

"Miss Richards has not been there," he continued, "and I doubt whether she would ever return. Not only is the aunt mad, she's vindictive, spiteful, and cruel. As a matter of fact, I asked the footman there if a Miss Richards had paid a call on Lady Ormstead, and his denial was most emphatic."

Dr. Ross shook his head. "I must confess, I was pinning my hopes on the aunt, for, quite honestly, I cannot think of where else she could have gone. I don't suppose she had much money with her?"

"Mama would know the answer to that, but I would doubt it." Lord Umber turned to David. "Can your legal mind think of anything that we laymen have missed?"

David shrugged his shoulders. "It's a mystery . . . an absolute mystery. Wait, it's just an idea, but has she made any particular friends since she has been in London? Someone she would trust enough to turn to, or want to confide in? It is always possible that she is enjoying a comfortable gossip and doesn't realize the time."

Lord Umber shook his head slowly. "She would have sent word to Mama that she had been detained had that been the case, unless I am much mistaken about her character, for she would not want to cause Mama any unnecessary worry. No, I think it's possible that she has met with an accident." A frown gathered on his brow as he spoke, the suggestion he had just made not at all to his liking. He dismissed it with another shake of his head. "Paul, I hate to sound so disbelieving, but are you absolutely sure nothing occurred this morning that we should know about? Her disappearance doesn't make sense otherwise. . . ." He broke off as the butler entered, bearing a tray which he carefully placed on a side table. "Thank you, Sims, that will be all." He gestured to his guests to help themselves as he poured himself a large brandy. Normally, he did not imbibe during the day, but this latest news of Felicia had upset him. He recalled the conversation they had at breakfast, but could think of nothing he said that would have caused her to run away. "Well, Paul?"

"Absolutely not, Ian," he answered emphatically. If he thought, for one moment that Felicia's disappearance had anything to do with what he only suspected were her true feelings for Lord Umber, he knew he would say something. But he didn't, and so he decided it was best to say nothing. He glanced at David, as though looking for support, but as a discreet tapping at the door ended the conversation, he sipped at his drink while Lord Umber bade the butler enter.

"Excuse me, your lordship," Sims said tentatively. "Lady Barbara Whitelaw is here, asking to see Lady Louisa."

The three men looked at each other in surprise. "Do you think Miss Richards . . . ?" Paul began.

"Hardly," Lord Umber said, remembering the comtempt that had unconsciously crept into Felicia's voice that morning as they talked of Lady Barbara. "Even so, I will see her, just in case she has some news." He turned to Sims. "Show her into the rose room. I will join her shortly."

"Is it likely that she would pay a social call on Lady Louisa?" Paul asked skeptically.

"No," David answered with a short laugh. "Not ordinarily. But, methinks that her Mama is determined to make Ian come up to scratch and so is pushing Lady Barbara into an uneasy alliance with Ian's Mama."

"Your logical mind has probably found the correct answer, David. If you will both excuse me, it will take but a few minutes to confirm what you suspect and I will be right back." Lord Umber strode from the room, leaving a heavy silence in his wake.

Lady Barbara was pacing the room nervously, the beauty of her surroundings completely ignored as she pondered her next step. It had seemed so simple this morning, but now she was actually here, the piece of information she wanted to relay about Felicia seemed petty and insignificant. Would Lady Louisa really think any the worse of her protoégée if she were told that Felicia's father was a gambler? But what if she knew already? For the only time in her life, Lady Barbara was daunted. How could she have been so stupid as to imagine that anyone would listen to her and not suspect an ulterior motive. For the first time she saw herself as others might see her and shuddered. Why, she appeared quite spiteful.

Deciding that it would be easier to make her excuses to the butler and leave, rather than face Lady Louisa, she moved over to the bell rope and gave it a sharp tug. The door opened and as she turned she said, "I am afraid I cannot wait . . ." She froze in dismay as she saw that Lord Umber stood in the doorway. "Why, Lord Umber," she said feebly. "What a surprise!"

"I am sorry to have kept you waiting, Lady Barbara,"

he said pleasantly. "My mother is indisposed. Can I help in any way?"

"No . . . no . . . that is . . . I . . . I only came to . . . to . . ." she broke off lamely and tapped her foot in anguish. This was not part of her plan at all. And now, to be so completely disarmed by his presence. His close proximity caused a flutter in her heart. He really was indecently handsome and dressed to perfection. What a striking couple they would make! She raised a limpid gaze to him and smiled flirtatiously. "I was passing and thought to inquire after Lady Louisa's health. She is all right, is she not?"

"Apart from a slight agitation of nerves, perfectly well, thank you," Lord Umber answered, hiding his disappointment that she did not have any news of Felicia. Yet he was puzzled by her sudden interest in his mother's welfare. "And your indisposition? I hope that you are entirely recovered." His voice was bland.

Lady Barbara flushed a dull red at this. "Yes. Yes," she answered hastily, not enjoying the reference to her note. "The physician said it was brought about by too many late nights. But Mama and I wondered about Lady Louisa when we saw Miss Richards in Harley Street this morning. We wondered if she . . . she . . ."

"What time was this?" Lord Umber interrupted sharply.

Lady Barbara looked at him in surprise. "Why, I suppose it must have been past eleven. I cannot say for certain."

She must have just left Paul then, he thought. "You didn't happen to notice which direction she took, or whether she was with anyone?"

What odd questions he was asking, to be sure, and with such concern. Lady Barbara looked at him acutely. "Why? Has something happened to her?" Her voice was harsh as a feeling of jealousy swept over her. What could she do to elicit such consideration from him?

"Not to my knowledge," he answered evasively. " 'Tis merely that Mama is slightly perturbed that Miss Richards might have lost her way. She was out on an errand, and Mama is convinced that Miss Richards misunderstood her directions."

"She can always hail a hansom," Lady Barbara said in disdain. "It is what I would do if I found myself in strange surroundings."

"Quite so, Lady Barbara. But then you are exceptionally practical, are you not?"

"Immeasurably more than Miss Richards, or her father, it would seem," she said spitefully, regretting the words instantly.

"Whatever do you mean, Lady Barbara?" Lord Umber asked in a dangerously quiet voice.

"Nothing. Nothing. 'Twas something that Mama heard about Mr. Richards that led me to believe he was . . ."

"Gossip, you mean?" Lord Umber said, not allowing her to finish.

Goaded beyond endurance as she saw her chances of snaring the biggest prize on the marriage market dissolve, she was driven to snap back sacastically. "Hardly. It appears to be a well-known fact that her father was a gambler. I am surprised that neither you nor Lady Louisa are aware of it."

"I fail to see why that piece of information should provoke such a comment from you." He was exasperated by this turn in the conversation. "Miss Richards' family tree was not in question."

"Well, it should be," Lady Barbara retorted petulantly. "Anyway, I do not know where she was going, and frankly I do not care."

Lord Umber surveyed her cynically. What a self-centered little puss she had turned out to be! He was torn between feeling a slight disgust with himself for having encouraged her ambitions, and pity for her because of her inability to recognize their flirtation was at an end. Felicia had been quite right about Lady Barbara, he could see that now. She was nothing more than a scheming vixen. "I am sorry to hear you say that, Lady Barbara, for you are talking of the lady I intend to marry." He stopped himself, surprised by his own words, but liked them enough to repeat them.

Lady Barbara looked at him aghast. "Ma . . . ma . . . marry?" she stuttered in astonishment. "You and Miss Ri . . . ? Why . . . why . . ." She turned away in an effort to compose herself. She simply could not believe that he meant what he had just said. It was impossible. Lord Umber marrying a nonentity, a gambler's daughter. She stamped her foot in frustration. Oh! How people would laugh at her now! She had been so confident that she could bring him up to scratch. With a supreme effort she squared her shoulders and forced herself to speak. "If . . . if you will excuse me, my lord, I will bid you good-day. Pray accept my . . . my felicitations." She walked proudly to the door and was gone before Lord Umber could move.

He was bemused by the turn of events, for until he had actually uttered those words, he had not been consciously aware of his feelings toward Felicia. Poor Lady Barbara, what a shock it must have been for her. His eyes rested heavily on the open door as his thoughts returned to Felicia. He must find her quickly, before Lady Barbara had time to spread any malicious gossip.

What a coil he had caused. What if Felicia should turn him down? He dismissed that thought and any idea that the problems facing him would be insurmountable. Somehow, he would succeed.

For someone who had been in the depth of despair a few moments ago, the realization of his love had worked like a magic potion. He reentered the library with a jaunty step and his normal haughty demeanor had been replaced by one of amusement.

His friends ceased their low-toned conversation on his arrival and, emboldened by his triumphant air, asked, "She is with Lady Barbara?"

He beamed at them happily. "No. No. But when I find her, I am going to marry her." The fact that he made no sense did not bother him.

"What! Congratulations!" they said in unison, his high spirits infecting them momentarily.

David was the first one to turn to more practical things. "At the risk of putting a damper on the proceedings, gentlemen, I feel that this might be an appropriate moment to deliver my news."

Lord Umber looked at him, an expression of fashionable boredom cloaking his eyes. "Well?" he inquired lazily.

"Before you make a complete cake of yourself, Ian, I think you should seek the permission of Miss Richards' grandfather."

"Who is that, David?" Dr. Ross asked sharply. "Miss Richards herself does not know."

"Exactly. That is why I came here this afternoon. The 'old man' did not feel equal to the task and asked me to present his case to Miss Richards."

Lord Umber looked at David questioningly. There was only one person whom David referred to as the 'old man.'

David nodded. "Yes, Ian, you are quite right. Her grandfather is none other than Lord Davenport."

Lord Umber's astonishment was plain. "Lord Davenport, David? How did this come about? One minute Miss Richards is a penniless orphan. The next she has acquired a title and family. My mind is befuddled."

"I was talking over the case with him this morning and he supplied the answer. Andrew Davenport, whom we knew as Andrew Richards, was his youngest son. When Andrew married into the 'trade,' Lord Davenport cut him off without a penny."

"How nonsensical," Lord Umber said irritably.

"Quite," David concurred. "Unfortunately, that was the case and not something Lord Davenport regretted doing for several years. By which time, Andrew and Arabella had disappeared without trace. The only connection Lord Davenport had was Lady Ormstead. When he approached her, she flatly denied knowing anything that could help him. She claimed that she had not heard from them in years. He continued his search, never suspecting that his son had changed his name."

"Surely Lady Ormstead knew?" Lord Umber asked. "Why did she not volunteer the information?"

"Jealousy, Ian, jealousy," Dr. Ross replied. "Do you not see that once she told her sister that Lord Davenport was willing, nay anxious to put the past behind them and start afresh, it would put Arabella in a higher social position than herself. My God!" he ejaculated, "what a sick, convoluted mind Lady Ormstead has. No wonder Miss Richards tried to suppress all memories of her."

The three men looked at each other in amazement.

To break the uncomfortable silence, Dr. Ross said to Lord Umber, "I was right then, Ian. Miss Richards is well-connected."

Lord Umber smiled. "But in the end, Paul, it would have made no difference to me." He cast a rueful look at David. "And, in some ways, I wish it weren't so, for now I have to persuade Lord Davenport that I am a worthy suitor for his granddaughter's hand."

"Let us not jump ahead of ourselves," David said hastily. "First, I must inform Lord Davenport that Miss Richards is missing, then we must find her. Frankly, I wouldn't know where to begin." He shook his head. "Excuse me, my patron is anxious for news. I shall be in my chambers late tonight, if you need to contact me. Otherwise, I will call first thing in the morning for news."

"Very good, David. I appreciate your help." A note of despondency crept into Lord Umber's voice as he envisaged the difficulties ahead. He could not countenance sitting at home waiting for Felicia to contact his mother, yet, as David had just said, where did one begin to search for a young girl in London.

He was so deeply engrossed in his thoughts that he neither noticed David leaving, nor the look of sympathy Dr. Ross gave him. He snapped his fingers as an idea came to him. "Those relatives in Manchester, Paul, do you think she would go to them?"

Dr. Ross looked sheepish, wishing once again that he had not invented them. If he had known then what he knew now of Lord Umber's intentions towards Felicia, he would have acted far differently. "To be quite honest with you, Ian, Miss Richards does not have any relatives there. It was something I said in haste, in an effort to comply with her request that you and Lady Louisa be kept in ignorance of the true facts." He looked at Lord Umber apologetically. "You see, Miss Richards felt that you would be compelled to deal with her aunt if you knew the full details of the treatment she suffered whilst living at Graystones, but, more importantly, she did not want your pity. I am sorry I had to go to the lengths I did to mislead you, Ian."

"I appreciate your loyalty to your patient, Paul," Lord Umber said, wearily brushing a hand across his brow. "But it means we are right back where we started. Where on earth can she be?"

Fifteen

David's interview with Lord Davenport had been short. The elderly judge, although extremely disappointed that his granddaughter could not be restored to him immediately, was inclined to take a more optimistic view of her disappearance.

"You know how it is with young people nowadays, David, they get caught up in what they are doing and quite forget about time. No. No. It is my contention that she is on her way back to Lady Louisa's at this very moment and we shall be hearing from Lord Umber momentarily."

David had done nothing to dissuade Lord Davenport to the contrary, feeling that it was far better for the old man to be comfortable with his thoughts than fretting over the possibility that Felicia could have met with a serious accident.

As he entered his own chambers, he frowned to see a light still burning in his senior clerk's cubicle. The hour was far too advanced for anyone to be still working, yet it was unlike Adams to leave his lamp lit. He closed the outer door noisily, and Adams quickly appeared.

"Why, Adams, whatever are you doing here so late?" he asked in surprise.

"Mr. Burton," Adams whispered hoarsely in relief. "I am so glad you're here. I didn't know where to find you, but knew you would return to your chambers at some point."

"Is something wrong? I swear I have never seen you looking so agitated."

His clerk, normally immaculate in his dress, looked crumpled, and his silver hair was tousled. Aware that his appearance was lacking its normal precision, Adams attempted to straighten himself.

"I do apologize, Mr. Burton," he said earnestly. "I must have drowsed off. The fact is that a policeman by the name of Jack Walsh has been here, claiming to have news as to the whereabouts of a certain Miss Richards. His attitude made me suspicious and so . . ."

"Miss Richards, did you say, Adams?" David asked. "Where is this Mr. Walsh? I must see him at once."

"He left over an hour ago. Said he couldn't wait a minute longer, especially as he was beginning to think it all bam that you really knew her. I'm afraid that as I didn't recognize the name myself, I was inclined to agree with him. It was only after he left that I started to think it all odd and so decided to wait for you. I hope I have done the correct thing."

David stared at his clerk in dismay. "Did he say where Miss Richards was, Adams?"

"Newgate, Mr. Burton. Up on a charge of purse-snatching."

David's dismay turned to disbelief. "Did he not leave a letter of explanation or details of how we could reach Miss Richards?"

Adams shook his head slowly. "He refused to leave a note that Miss Richards had written. He said that if you wanted to see her you could go to Newgate in the morning and ask for Mistress James."

"That panderer!" David exclaimed furiously. "Come, Adams, we have not a moment to lose. Bring all the spare cash we have, for I know that gold is the only language those guardians of justice understand, and it is imperative that we get Miss Richards out of that hell-hole immediately." He paced the room angrily, at the same time trying to think clearly. He wondered briefly whether he should notify either Lord Davenport or Ian of this latest development, before deciding that it would be better to see Felicia first and find out the truth surrounding her arrest. He did not for a moment believe there was any truth to the charge and deemed it wiser to wait until he had all the details before alarming anyone unnecessarily, especially Ian. He did not need any great imagination to know how he would react.

The most important person at this precise moment was Felicia, and his main objective was, quite obviously, to wrest her away from Mistress James who was, without doubt, the meanest of all jailors in the woman's section.

"I'm ready, Mr. Burton," Adams said, reappearing

from his cubicle. "I have found nearly one hundred guineas. Will that be sufficient?"

David laughed harshly. "Mistress James would kill for twenty. Yes, Adams, I think we will have enough to free Miss Richards."

David's automatic assumption that Adams would accompany him on this mission pleased the clerk. He had worked with David for the past six years and in that time had learned to respect not only David's fine legal mind, but also the compassion he showed to the underprivileged. However, David's insistence on defending the more unsavory criminals had horrified Adams in the beginning and, although he had grown accustomed to dealing with these characters when they came to Lincoln's Inn, he never felt easy when David spent any length of time at Newgate or The Fleet interviewing a prospective client.

Adams was puzzled by the sudden interest David was showing in this Miss Richards, for until a few minutes ago he had never heard of her. Yet David's reaction to the news that she was in Newgate was enough to confirm she was important. He waited until they were safely ensconced in a cab and well on the way to the prison before he broached the subject.

"Who is this Miss Richards, Mr. Burton?"

David scrutinized his clerk in the dim glow shed by the carriage light before answering slowly. "I know I can rely on your discretion, Adams, else I would not have asked you to accompany me. . . ."

Adams coughed deprecatingly. "Quite so, Mr. Burton."

"Miss Richards is actually Lord Davenport's granddaughter."

There was no mistaking the astonishment that Adams experienced at this piece of news. His mouth fell open as he gaped wordlessly at David.

"There is no doubt in my mind that Miss Richards has been wrongfully accused . . . that she is suffering needlessly because of some grave error. However, I think you can see that it would serve no useful purpose to air the truth about Lord Davenport's connection to Miss Richards. He has too many detractors who would give a great deal to be able to use that information against him. I hope that between us, we can finesse Mistress James into releasing Miss Richards into our custody tonight. Then tomorrow I can investigate the charges against her more fully and mayhap persuade the complainant to drop them. It would be fatal if Miss Richards had to appear in court."

Adams nodded understandingly. "You can rely on me to do all that is necessary, Mr. Burton. I have dealt with Mistress James a few times and found that after a few pulls at the gin bottle she can be quite amenable."

Both men fell into a thoughtful silence which was only broken by the steady clip-clop of the horse drawing their carriage.

When, at last, they arrived outside the massive gates of the prison, Adams gave the driver instructions to wait. The man agreed, but only after much grumbling and the promise of extra money for his patience.

"Nice work," David said warmly, as he rang the bell at the forbidding entrance. "If all goes well, we should be out of here in less than fifteen minutes."

A shaft of light shone through a crack in the door and the sounds of someone pulling back an iron bar could be heard. But instead of the gates being opened, a small piece of steel that covered the peephole was pushed back, and David found himself being observed by a pair of eyes.

"Yes?" a gruff voice inquired. "What can be done ter 'elp yer at this time of night?"

"Who is this?" David asked in his well-modulated voice. He knew most of the guards at Newgate and anticipated little difficulty in gaining admittance. "It is Mr. Burton here, seeking an interview with Mistress James." There was a long pause, and David could feel the eyes raking him up and down. "Come on, my good man," he continued with just a touch of irritation. "If you dally any longer, Mistress James will have retired for the night."

"All in good time, sir, all in good time. I can't be letting everybody in, just because they ask. It's my duty to check on all personages entering these 'ere portals." With seemingly slow, ponderous movements, the guard slid back the peephole cover and proceeded to draw the bolts and chains. Finally, one door was swung open, and David and Adams entered.

"Oh! It's you, Watson," David said, recognizing the dour-faced guard instantly. "We will not be long, so wait for us to return."

Watson bowed obsequiously, managing at the same time to hold out his hand. "Of course, Mr. Burton. And I'm sorry to 'ave kept you waiting. Only you can't be too sure nowadays and can't take enough precautions. Got to look at everyone, I 'as."

Adams slid a coin into the outstretched hand as he followed David across the courtyard. "At this rate, I wonder if we have enough funds," he commented lightly. "Let us hope you are right about Mistress James."

David laughed wryly at this sally. By now they had reached the isolated women's section. As they entered, the babble of wailing voices that assailed their ears was awe-inspiring and the stench was abominable. Adams looked at David apprehensively.

"Thank goodness, you had the foresight to wait for me to return tonight," David said grimly. "The very idea that Miss Richards would be forced to spend a night here is unthinkable." He rapped his cane loudly on a door.

"Who's there?" a female voice shouted out rudely. "And what d'yer want?"

"Fetch Mistress James," David commanded. "My business is with her."

The door was flung open and a woman of undiscernible age greeted them with a toothless grin. "And what can I do you for?" she cackled, smacking her thick lips across her gums. "Anyone who comes a-calling at this time of the night can only cause trouble in my book." She let out another shrill laugh and opened the door wider as she beckoned them in.

Adams stepped forward first and ignoring the smell that emanated from her said, "Mistress James, do you remember me? The name is Adams. I work for Mr. Burton."

David stepped into the light as though to confirm his clerk's statement.

"Oh! We are 'onored, aren't we just," Mistress James said raucously, dropping a mock curtsy. "The 'igh and mighty one 'isself. And ter think I almost didn't believe that Jack Walsh. Who'd 'ave thought that you would 'ave come. Your friend must really be important." A trickle of saliva ran out of the side of her mouth as she spoke and, with an unconscious movement, she brought the back of her filthy hand across her equally dirty mouth to wipe it off.

Both men looked away in disgust.

"We have come to take Miss Richards home," Adams said curtly. "We also want to know what the charges are that have been brought against her and by whom."

"Not so fast there, my boy. You can't just sweep in 'ere and make demands. I'm paid to do a job and I do my best, even though they're an ungrateful bunch of vermin." She gestured contemptuously towards the caged part of the prison. " 'Eathens, nothing but 'eathens." She spat into a receptacle on the floor and grinned in satisfaction as the globule fell squarely in the middle, floating for a moment before sinking.

"Mistress James," David said quietly. "I think you know my reputation, and you must realize that I would not demand you release a prisoner if it were outside the law. Miss Richards is not only a close friend of my family, she is also my client. As such, I am allowed to confer with her. If she has been brought before a judge for a hearing, then, no doubt, a date has been set for her trial." He paused as though waiting for an answer, but continued as the woman shook her head. "If, as I suspect, Miss Richards has been incarcerated without being properly charged, then you are outside the law and cannot refuse my request." He gambled that her knowledge of the law was scant and that she would believe him.

Adams, realizing what David was doing, smiled reassuringly at her. He could see she was wavering and so said quickly, "You will be well rewarded for the trouble we have put you to tonight." He jangled some coins suggestively in his hand. "And you need not fear that your compassion will be forgotten."

Muttering to herself, she waddled to the door and shouted into the inky blackness something that neither man could understand. As she returned to the center of the room she took a bottle out of a concealed pocket and, pulling the cork from the neck with her gums, proceeded to take a large swig. "Purely medicinal," she said sourly to her audience. "It's the ticker that's bad and always gets worse when I'm upset." She sat down heavily on a chair. "She'll be 'ere in a little while."

David felt the tension leave him at her words. One never knew how Mistress James would react to anything, and he had not been at all certain that they would succeed in persuading her to release Felicia. He put a hand to the back of his neck and massaged it gently. "And the records?"

Adams opened his hand briefly to expose the gold coins. Mistress James eyed them greedily.

"Aye. You can 'ave them as well." She pulled open a desk drawer and produced a grimy ledger and some equally grubby papers. She pushed the book across the table top toward Adams. "You'd best sign 'ere, just in case I needs the proof. It wouldn't do me reputation no good, if word leaked out I was too lenient with my prisoners."

Adams picked up a quill and, dipping it into an inkpot, signed his name with a flourish on the line indicated. As he handed her back the ledger he carefully counted out ten guineas and pushed these over toward her before taking the papers. He looked at them carefully and then passed them to David. "I would say they are the genuine ones." David nodded in agreement.

Mistress James was still staring at the pile of gold and shaking her head in disbelief. She had never seen so much money at one time, but with a cunning born of her background she knew there would be more for the asking. "And the same again for the girl," she whispered, "and no arguments, otherwise she goes right back downstairs."

The sounds of approaching people lent an urgency to her words and so, without protesting, David nodded laconically to Adams who counted out ten more coins. As both men turned towards the passageway, Mistress James swept the money into a dirty rag and hid the bundle in the folds of her skirt.

"And 'ere we 'ave Miss Prim-and-Proper," she crowed as Felicia appeared. "And thankful it is I am to be rid of her."

Felicia looked at David speechlessly for a moment before she realized that her ordeal was over. She shrugged off the arm of her jailor and walked towards him unsteadily. "Thank you, David," was all she could say. "Thank you."

Sixteen

*Dinner for Lady Louisa that night con-*sisted of dry biscuits. Her nervous stomach would not permit anything else. Lord Umber and Dr. Ross had not yet returned, and she did not expect them for a while. They had gotten the idea to visit all the hospitals in the vicinity of Harley Street to see if Felicia had been admitted as a patient, for somehow Ian had convinced himself that she had met with an accident.

Lady Louisa closed her eyes wearily. So much had happened so swiftly. The disclosure that Felicia's grandfather was Lord Davenport and that he had been searching for her family for years was gratifying, for this confirmed the suspicion that lady had had all along that Felicia was well-bred. But when Ian informed her that he had decided he wanted nothing more than to marry Felicia, she had felt compelled to point out to him that Felicia would need time to adjust to her new family, and that he simply could not assume that she would return his feelings. Also such talk was premature, for there was no guarantee that she would be found. The anguished look on his face after she had spoken had been heartrending and indicated that Felicia's disappearance had affected him as deeply as his father's death had. She wished she could comfort him, but knew there was little she could say to ease his mind. It was a nightmare they would all have to live through.

She must have dozed, for suddenly she was jerked awake by the sounds of knocking on the front door. She pulled herself upright and patted her cap straight as she waited for the footman to answer the summons. A few minutes later her son stood on the threshold of the salon, his pale, drawn face proof that he had been unsuccessful in his search.

Without a word, he crossed to the drink tray that stood on the sideboard and poured himself a good measure of brandy. He tossed this down and poured himself another before speaking.

"Mama . . . Mama . . ." he said helplessly. "The truth is I know not where to start looking. She has vanished without a trace."

"I know, son," Lady Louisa soothed. "I know. But we must not give up hope yet." She glanced up at the delicate, gold filigree clock on the mantle and was surprised to see that it was only eight o'clock. "There is still plenty of time for news tonight. Where is Paul?"

"He had some things to attend to, but he promised to look in later on to check on you," he answered bleakly. He paced the room like a caged animal, stopping by the fireplace to kick the coals. "What else can I do? Whom can I approach? Where can I go? Damn, damn, damn." He talked to himself, oblivious to his mother's presence. "I know she is behind it. I know it." He stopped abruptly and turned towards Lady Louisa with a triumphant expression on his face. "And I intend seeing her this very instant." He tugged the bell rope impatiently.

Sims entered immediately. "Yes, my lord?"

"Order my carriage for me," he instructed.

"Where . . . where are you going, Ian?" Lady Louisa asked hesitantly. She had never seen her son this angry before; it seemed to her that he was fairly spitting with rage.

"To Lady Ormstead's. I am going to force her to tell me what she had done with Miss Richards, for I am as certain as I can be that she is responsible for her disappearance."

"But, Ian," Lady Louisa protested feebly, "you cannot force yourself on anybody at this time of night. And . . . and besides, she may not be in."

"If that is the case, I will wait for her. No, Mama, my mind is set. I cannot sit here waiting for something to happen. It is unthinkable."

"Then you must do as you suggest," Lady Louisa answered with a calmness she did not feel. The frustration and forlornness her son was experiencing was too painful to watch and, although she was apprehensive about what he would say to this Lady Ormstead, she knew she was powerless to prevent him from going. "Leave her direction with Sims," was all she said. "And I will send word to you, should I hear anything."

Lord Umber nodded grimly and strode from the room, his features hardened into a ruthless expression.

Lady Louisa rose from her chair unsteadily, her sense of frustration as complete as her son's. Where could Felicia have gone? She shook her head in bewilderment.

She started nervously as she heard the knocker sound again, and waited anxiously for Sims to announce the visitor. She heard the low murmuring of voices as people entered the hallway and she gave a joyous cry as she recognized the light tones of Felicia. Unable to wait for Sims to do his duty, she opened the door and quickly stepped out into the hallway.

"Felicia," she exclaimed jubilantly. "My dear child!" Seconds later she was embracing Felicia, tears of relief falling down her cheeks. "Oh! Felicia, how glad I am to see you." She stood back and looked her up and down, searching for outward signs of injury. Finding none, she asked, "You are not hurt?"

Felicia shook her head, too emotionally drained to speak. She glanced at David beseechingly.

Lady Louisa, suddenly realizing where she was, relinquished her hold on Felicia. "Shall we go into the salon? I am sure we will be more comfortable there." She led the way, putting her arm through Felicia's, leaving David and Adams to follow.

Once they were all seated and David had made the necessary introduction of Adams to Lady Louisa, a silence fell.

"I . . . I . . . am sorry to have caused such a stir," Felicia said softly, aware that Lady Louisa was waiting for her to speak. "It's . . . it's been such a . . ."

"That you have been restored to me is sufficient for the moment," Lady Louisa said swiftly, seeing the distress on Felicia's face. "Tomorrow is soon enough to talk."

David nodded his approval. "Your thoughtfulness is appreciated, I am sure, Lady Louisa. Miss Richards has been through an excruciating experience." He smiled at Felicia encouragingly. "She wanted to come here tonight, preferring to wait until the morrow to meet her grandfather."

Felicia looked at Lady Louisa candidly, her blue eyes enormous with strain. "I cannot think properly this evening, so much has happened and I know . . . I know I have to go to Lord Davenport's tomorrow, but I wanted nothing more than to sleep in familiar surroundings tonight."

"My dear, I would not want it any other way. You are always welcome here, you know that. Come, let me put you to bed." Lady Louisa turned to David and Adams. "I beg that you wait for me to return. I will not keep you above a few minutes."

The door closed softly behind her, and David sat back tiredly. "Thank goodness that is behind us, Adams—though how Miss Richards is ever going to forget her experience at Newgate is beyond me. I swear the memory of Mistress James will be with *me* for a long time to come."

"She was certainly not a pretty sight tonight," Adams agreed. He stood up. "If you don't mind, Mr. Burton, I will be getting along now. I dare say my missus will have given me up for dead long since."

"By Jove! I am sorry, Adams," David exclaimed. "I must confess I never gave her a thought. My thanks to you for all you have done tonight. I will see you in the morning."

"Yes, sir," Adams said as he reached the door. "Good night."

As good as her word, Lady Louisa reappeared soon after Adams' departure. "The poor girl is exhausted," she fussed. "I swear she fell asleep as soon as her head touched the pillow."

"I am not surprised to hear that," David replied. "Thank you for not creating a fuss, for that was one thing Miss Richards wanted to avoid."

"What did happen to her, David? I cannot stand the suspense a moment longer."

David regarded her pensively, uncertain whether he should divulge everything without Ian's presence. "It's a harrowing tale, which I would prefer to relate when Ian is here. Will he be in shortly?"

Lady Louisa clasped her hands together in annoyance. "Oh! Lordie me! I clean forgot. He went off to Lady Ormstead's, convinced she was at the root of Felicia's disappearance and determined to force her to talk. Excuse me, I must ask Sims to send a messenger there to let him know that Felicia is safe."

"I think it would be best for me to go, Lady Louisa. If Ian has gained admittance, then a great deal of discretion will be needed, for he was right. Lady Ormstead was indeed behind Miss Richards' misadventure."

"Oh no!" Lady Louisa said faintly, sitting down hastily. "Then you must get there before Ian loses his temper completely."

"Of course. I will return as soon as possible, but I must

stop in at Lord Davenport's for I have promised to give him word of his granddaughter."

"I shall look for you both within the hour, then."

However, it was nearly two hours before they returned and, if Lord Umber was relieved that Felicia was safely asleep upstairs, the scowl on his face belied his feelings.

"I am sorry we kept you waiting, Mama," he said, as he poured himself another drink, "but Lord Davenport insisted that we stay for supper. In the circumstances it seemed uncivil to refuse."

"I understand, Ian. Paul has been here, and he looked in on Felicia. He seemed quite satisfied that she was sleeping normally and said to tell you he would call first thing in the morning. Was . . . was Lord Davenport glad of your news, David?"

"Enormously, Lady Louisa. He wants to do what is best for Miss Rich . . . I mean, Lady Felicia, and feels that perhaps it will be best for her to prolong her stay with you until she has adjusted to the idea of belonging to a family again."

"How thoughtful of him, to be sure. He may be right, but I think we should ask Felicia in the morning what it is *she* wants to do. Mayhap we could invite Lord Davenport to luncheon, so they can become acquainted gradually." She glanced at her son. "Don't you agree, Ian?"

"Indeed, Mama, an excellent suggestion," he answered absently. "Mama, are you certain that Paul said she was all right? I mean, he didn't think that because she had suffered another shock she would lose her memory again?"

"He didn't mention that possibility, as I was unable to supply him with any of the details of her ordeal. He thought it best not to speculate."

"A wise doctor," David murmured before turning to Lord Umber. "Ian, I am sure Lady Louisa has waited long enough to hear the story. Do you want to listen to me again, or would you be more comfortable with the telling?"

"No, no, David. It is something you had best repeat. Excuse me, Mama, but my temper is on a very short rein at the moment. Pray disregard any oaths that you may hear me utter." He lapsed into an unhappy silence as he stared into the dancing flames of the fire.

He had paid scant attention to his mother's words of caution not to rush into proposing to Felicia, but the last hour spent in Lord Davenport's company had forced him to conclude that it would be most unfair of him to say aught until Felicia had had time to enjoy her new life. Now doubts were assailing him, for Lord Davenport had made it quite clear that he intended presenting Felicia to Society. How could he declare himself and deny her the opportunity of having what every young lady coveted— the romance of a Season in London. Yet, if he bided his time, it was always possible that she would form an attachment for some unworthy whelp. He let out an oath.

Lady Louisa looked at him anxiously, wondering what it was that was still bothering him. "I trust you left Lady Ormstead in one piece, Ian?" she asked lightly. There was something in his brooding expression that made her feel uneasy.

"I found him on the doorstep," David answered. "He had been quite unsuccessful in his attempt to wake up anyone in that house, even though he caused the devil of a commotion and had most of the neighbors complaining of the noise." He smiled reassuringly at Lady Louisa, trying to allay her fears. He, too, was concerned about Lord Umber, for the black mood of despair he was presently suffering had descended suddenly in the midst of their supper. It was difficult to console him, not knowing the cause.

"And well might she hide," Lord Umber said suddenly, "for this is the last night she will ever rest easy. I was correct in my assumption, Mama. She was indeed responsible for Lady Felicia's disappearance. . . ." He broke off, rage choking him into speechlessness.

David quickly broke in, sensing that Lord Umber's behavior was far more disturbing to Lady Louisa than the actual story of Felicia's plight would be. "The ugly truth is that Lady Felicia has spent the better part of today in Newgate prison because Lady Ormstead accused her of purse-snatching."

Lady Louisa sank back into the cushions as all the color drained from her cheeks. She felt strangely lightheaded as she absorbed this information, unwilling to believe her ears.

"The poor girl. The poor, dear, sweet girl. It is hardly any wonder she was so distraught tonight." With an effort she struggled into an upright position and fumbled for her purse. The room spun in front of her and, as she tried to focus on a low coffee table in front of her, she was suddenly aware of a pair of strong arms forcing her back on the chaise. Somewhere in the distance she could hear a bottle being uncorked and a quiet voice whispering instructions. Then the familiar odor of her smelling salts steadied her vision and the faintness that had threatened to overwhelm her receded.

"That's better," she heard her son say. "She will be all right in a moment."

"I am sorry, Ian. It never occurred to me that she would react so. Indeed, I would have held back if I had known."

"She had to know sometime, David, so don't be worrying yourself needlessly. And, I am sure my behavior affected her adversely." He smiled ruefully. "My indisposition must be due to the combined effect of knowing that I must wait to declare my 'honorable' intentions to Lady Felicia, and thinking of Lady Ormstead. Mama," he said as he patted her wrists lightly. "Mama, are you feeling better?"

Lady Louisa nodded. "Yes, thank heavens. I am sorry to be such a wet goose. I don't know what came over me. Please, David, continue."

"There is little else to say, except that I will settle the score with Lady Ormstead tomorrow."

Lord Umber broke in quickly as he saw an apprehensive look enter his mother's eye. "There is no need to worry that I shall interfere, Mama. I have already given my word to Lord Davenport and David that I will stay well away."

"That is a relief," Lady Louisa murmured faintly.

"And," David continued with a smile, "I will insure that she never attempts to see Lady Felicia again."

"Do you think she will listen to you?" Lady Louisa asked. "She sounds to me like a person who will do exactly as she wants and bully anyone who stands in her way."

"She will listen. Lord Davenport calls it blackmail, I merely regard it as tightening the purse-strings. You see, I control her late husband's estate, and consequently have to approve all her major expenses. . . ."

"Call it what you will," Lady Louisa laughed. "I approve of your plan entirely."

Seventeen

Felicia woke the next morning feeling refreshed. The horror of the previous day was still with her, but the security of being in familiar surroundings was reassuring. She refused to think of her aunt—indeed she couldn't do so without shaking—and David had been most insistent that she concentrate on the more positive happenings of the previous day. Especially on the fact that her grandfather wanted her to live with him.

She tried to imagine what he would be like, but it was difficult as the face of Lord Umber kept intruding. If the truth were known, she would be far happier away from London, away from anything that would remind her of him. However, David had made it quite clear that her grandfather wanted to present her at Court and let the world know that he had found a part of his family he had given up for lost years ago.

Well, she would do her best to please the old man, but she knew it would not be easy. Her heart was not ready for enjoyment of that kind.

Yesterday, to keep her mind from the terrors of Newgate, she had spent hours imagining what life with Lord Umber would be like. She had fantasized at great length about the richness of their life together and how, between them, they would expand his charity program to all parts of England.

This morning she could laugh at those dreams, but she did not discount them, for one day she might well find herself in a position to give help on her own.

The usual morning sounds of the giggling housemaids and whistling footmen all busying themselves about their chores seemed immensely satisfying today, and she lay back in her bed and listened to them with pleasure. How much we all take for granted, she mused, when in reality everything we do or see should be treated as something special.

The door opened quietly, and Lady Louisa's maid peeked in. "Good morning, miss, Madam was wondering if you felt well enough to join her for some hot chocolate. She is in her bedroom."

"Of course I do, Lucy. Tell her I will be right in." Quickly she swung her legs onto the floor and wriggled her toes into a pair of fur-lined slippers. Reaching over, she picked up her robe, which was on a near-by chair, slipped it on, tying the belt neatly around her waist. She hurried along the cold corridor and tapped lightly on Lady Louisa's door before entering. "Good morning, Lady Louisa," she said smiling. "I cannot tell you how good it is to see you."

"My dear Felicia," Lady Louisa fluttered. "The very sight of you looking so well makes me feel immeasurably happier. I swear, if I had not known that you had been through a terrible ordeal, I would never have guessed."

Felicia laughed. "I am just following David's orders. He instructed me to think of all the nice things that have happened to me. And . . . and . . ." she paused before continuing diffidently, "you certainly have been the nicest."

"You flatter me, child. You have been far more beneficial for me than I for you. But, I am determined not to argue today. There is much to be done."

"I . . . I know, but I am finding it difficult to realize that I do indeed have a home and a grandfather. Actually. I am quite terrified at the prospect."

"As . suspected you might be, Felicia, and so, if you agree, I thought to invite Lord Davenport to have luncheon with us so that you may meet him without too much strain. And, if you like, you can stay here for a while longer and visit with your grandfather as much as you want, until you feel ready to move in with him."

Felicia sat down thoughtfully. The temptation to stay was enormous, for she would certainly see Lord Umber. But as she doubted the suitability of that idea, she decided regretfully that it would be best to make a clean and swift break. "I . . . I . . . think, I would prefer to . . . I mean . . . maybe it would be best for me to send word to grandfather to expect me this afternoon. It is not that I don't want to stay here, Lady Louisa . . ."

"Say no more, Felicia. I do understand. And it is not as though you are moving to the other end of England. I shall make it my business to see as much of you as possible. I am sure Lord Davenport will not object."

"Thank you," Felicia said gratefully. "I know it is silly to feel apprehensive, for David assures me that he is quite a mellow person now and is most anxious for me to live with him."

"I shall order the carriage for you at three then. That should give you plenty of time to ready yourself. I will ask Lucy to supervise the packing of your trunks."

"And that will give you plenty of time to tally up how much I must owe you for all the lovely gowns you have bought me," Felicia teased. "I suspect that once I tell grandfather about them he will insist on paying you back every farthing."

"Away with you, you nonsensical child, I would not dream of appearing to be a penny-pinching person. And, if you don't mention it, he will never think to ask. Men are all the same."

Except your son, Felicia thought as she returned to her room. She dressed quickly in front of the fire, determinedly pushing away thoughts of Lord Umber. Instead, she started to make a mental list of those she should bid farewell. Her toilette complete, she hurried downstairs to start this task.

The first person she encountered was Sims and, having thanked him prettily for the many kindnesses he had shown her, she turned to go downstairs to the kitchen. As she did so, the sound of Lord Umber's voice reached her. She stood still, unable to stop the sudden tremble in her knees, and watched him descend into the hallway. He looked tired and irritable, and she wondered if he had had a late night. She had been secretly disappointed by his ab-

sence last night when David had restored her to Lady
Louisa, for she had taken it as an indication that he had
not been worried over her disappearance. So, feigning a
casualness she did not feel, she stepped forward to greet
him.

"Ah! Lord Umber. The very person I was looking for.
I want to bid you farewell, for as you may know I go to
my grandfather's today."

Lord Umber stared down at her, unable to believe that
she was actually standing in front of him with an attitude
of total unconcern and looking none the worse for her ad-
venture. All night he had been haunted by dreams of the
terrible things that could have happened to her had David
not rescued her. Something in him snapped and all the
pent-up frustration of the last twenty-four hours burst out
of him like water gushing from a burst dam.

Ignoring her outstretched hand he said in clipped, angry tones, "Do you realize the anxiety Mama suffered?
Have you any conception of the havoc you wrought here
yesterday by your thoughtlessness?"

"But . . . but you don't understand," Felicia started to
say.

"No, I don't, *Lady* Felicia," Lord Umber interrupted.
"All I can hope is that your grandfather will drum some
sense into you. And may the first lesson he teaches you be
that you never, *never* walk abroad alone. Of all the
empty-headed actions I have ever heard of . . . why . . .
why that has to rank as one of the more inane. Whatever
were you doing in Blackfriars would be a question I
would ask you if I were your grandfather." He bowed
perfunctorily. "As you say, Lady Felicia, good-bye." He
turned and stalked out of the front door, unaware of the

gaping countenance of the footman who had witnessed his outburst.

Hurt and bewildered by his attitude, Felicia ran upstairs and sought the sanctury of her own room. Dismissing a chambermaid who was putting the final pieces of tissue paper in her trunk, she threw herself on the bed and gave way to the tears Lord Umber's words had induced. Finally, exhausted, she rose and studied her face in the mirror. Fortunately, apart from the reddened eyes, there was no other visible sign of how she spent the last ten minutes. Moving over to the washstand, she quickly splashed some cold water into the basin and dabbed her eyes carefully.

She felt a strange calm, almost a relief. In many ways it would be easier to leave Lady Louisa's now, knowing that Lord Umber thought so little of her. If she tried hard, maybe she could put her feelings for him to one side and possibly, one day, she would find that she neither ached to be near him, nor remembered the way one side of his mouth always crinkled when he smiled at one of her sallies. It was foolish to be so dramatic as to suppose one's heart broke, her's was merely cracked. She would come about, she had no choice.

She took her leave of Lady Louisa quickly, neither of them wanting to prolong the unhappy moment. Dr. Ross, who had visited them earlier that morning, had left some medicine for Lady Louisa in case she needed something to steady her nerves. He had also spent a long time with Felicia, drawing out of her every single detail of her ordeal. It had not been pleasant for her, but as he had said, it was far better to talk about something that unpleasant than to try and blank it from the mind.

She smiled appreciatively to herself at his philosophy. He was an eccentric young doctor, but, at least for her, effective.

"I have been here four days, Rufus, four whole days, and I feel as though I am in another world," Felicia whispered forlornly to the Irish wolfhound at her feet. The steady thumping of his tail on the soil indicated the intense pleasure he was experiencing as she stroked his neck. She stopped fondling him for a moment, but resumed when he whined and rested his head appealingly in her lap. "One more time, Rufus, and then I must go inside for Lady Louisa will be here shortly."

She was sitting in the small garden at the back of her grandfather's impressive house in Eaton Square. The warm, morning sunlight filtered through the trees, casting prancing shadows on the new grass. It was an idyllic spot for daydreaming, yet Felicia's sad expression was a sharp contrast to the brightness of the day.

Her grandfather was a dear old man, and she found it difficult to believe that he had been capable of turning his youngest son out for marrying beneath him. She had no thought that she would like him for that very reason, but she had been wrong.

He was anxious to insure she enjoyed herself, but as yet had been unable to adjust his lifestyle to incorporate one as young as she. He had been a widower too long to be entirely at ease in a woman's company, preferring to spend his leisure hours with his cronies at one of his clubs.

Felicia understood this, but after the activity of Lady Louisa's household, she still felt lost and lonely. Her maid companion was Rufus who had adopted her the moment she had arrived. Even her grandfather had been amazed by the dog's attitude. In four days the dog had become her devoted slave and closest confidant.

There had been no word from Lord Umber, and she had not really expected any. She had refrained from asking David for news when he had visited her, and he had not offered any. In fact, the reason for his visit had been to dissipate any fears she might still harbor about her aunt. He had come to report the outcome of his interview with her.

"She has already left for Graystones and will not return to London ever again."

"However did you persuade her to go?" Felicia asked. "She was quite adamant about spending the Season here, and even more determined to see Wendy safely settled."

"She succeeded in the latter. I believe an elderly gentleman took a fancy to your cousin, and the wedding is set for July. Someone by the name of Brown."

"A Mr. Brown?" Felicia queried. "Whoever is that? He does not sound as though his consequence is very large."

David laughed. "No, but in the circumstances I am certain that Lady Ormstead was happy enough to accept his offer, as I do not think that her daughter will receive another."

"And . . . and you are quite sure that I will never have to see her again?"

"Absolutely," David assured her. "You see, my law firm controls her late husband's estate. It's a small account and one that I have never bothered with before; Adams has always approved every expense in the past. As of today, however, I have put myself in charge, and she will have to seek my approval for any monies she may find herself in need of. . . ."

Felicia clapped her hands in delight. "So you would know immediately if she asks for a large sum of money, or if she planned to come to London?"

"Exactly. I think you can safely assume, Lady Felicia, that unless you want to visit her at Graystones, you need never see her again. And Wendy's marriage to Mr. Brown will insure that she never mingles in the society that you will be in. . . ."

"I am tempted to feel sorry for her, David, for it sounds as though she will lead a very dull life. Not a bit as she imagined it would be—full of parties and fun."

"Life seldom works out as we hope," David replied, "but sooner or later we seem to adjust to what we have."

"You are right, of course," Felicia said quickly. "And I suppose I am the best example."

He had taken his leave shortly after, and Felicia had spent a miserable hour wondering if David's last remark had been a veiled hint about Lord Umber.

She felt Rufus stiffen and looked up quickly to see who was approaching. It was Lady Louisa. Commanding Rufus to be still, she rose from her seat and warmly embraced her former employer.

Lady Louisa looked at Felicia sharply. There were dark rings under her eyes, and her cheeks had lost their rosy glow. "What ails you, child?" she chided gently. "You do not seem up to par."

"I am well enough," Felicia replied ruefully. "Although I do miss living at Berkeley Square. Grandfather tries to make me feel at home, but this really is such a masculine house."

"You must visit me often then, Felicia," Lady Louisa replied gently. "And see if you cannot persuade Lord Davenport to let you redecorate some of the rooms here. That should help a lot."

Felicia nodded. "He has already suggested that, but somehow, it seems unfair to alter an atmosphere he is quite content with. No. I am sure I shall become used to it." She turned away, wondering if she dare ask after Lord Umber. She coughed lightly. "And . . . and, Lord Umber. How is he?"

Lady Louisa sank onto a bench and patted the space beside her. "Come, sit down."

Felicia obeyed, nervously twisting a leaf in her fingers, aware that Lady Louisa was studying her face.

"I don't know, Felicia," she answered finally. "I really don't know what has gotten into him. He appears well enough, but he has changed."

"Changed, ma'am? In what way?"

"His temper for one thing. It always is at the boil. And . . . and he has started to drink so heavily. I hate to say this about my son, but it's as though he has stopped caring."

Saddened by this information, Felicia made a consoling sound before saying timidly, "Perhaps he has been gambling too heavily . . . losing too much money. I . . . I know that papa would become morose and difficult when that happened."

"I don't think so, at least no more than usual, otherwise word would have reached me. I must confess I am at a loss to know what to think."

"It . . . it is presumptuous of me to suggest it, but mayhap Lady Barbara turned him down." Even as she spoke, it seemed as though someone were twisting a knife in her heart, the pain her words caused was so intense.

"No. Not Lady Barbara, but it is a possibility that he is suffering because he has hurt someone he really cares for."

"Oh!" Felicia said faintly. "I am sorry. Maybe his condition will improve when he gets over his embarrassment. Mama always said that men recover from affairs of the heart far more quickly than we women." She looked away so that Lady Louisa would not see the anguished look she knew was in her eyes.

Lady Louisa looked grave. "I think this is more serious than that, for you see he lost his temper quite unnecessarily with this particular lady and now seems incapable of knowing how to apologize. It's all so silly, isn't it?"

Felicia felt herself blushing and nodded mutely in answer to the question.

"He also confessed to me, Felicia, that he treated you abominably. Would you agree to see him now, so that he can make amends?" She saw Felicia's look of hesitation and quickly pressed on. "He is waiting inside for my signal. If I do not give it, then he will leave . . . but. . . ."

Any doubts Lady Louisa had about Felicia's feelings toward her son were quickly swept away by the rapturous look that spread across Felicia's face at her words. She rose hastily and waving her handkerchief to Lord Umber, hurried past him into the house, well satisfied with the part she had played that morning.

Felicia kept her gaze down to the grass, too nervous to

look up. She reached out wildly to hold Rufus, who had started to growl again and murmured something to him. It was enough to reassure him that a friend approached, for he sank back on his haunches and started to wag his tail. Felicia felt someone sit down beside her and her heart started to thump wildly.

"I am sorry for my untimely show of temper, Felicia," the contrite voice said. "And I thank you for being so gracious as to receive me this morning." His hand closed over her fingers as he lifted them to his lips. He kissed each one gently, sending thrill after thrill coursing through her. "Am I forgiven?" he asked huskily.

"Forgiven, my lord?" she whispered. "Why there is nothing to forgive." She made a feeble effort to disengage her hand from his clasp, but his grip tightened and, instead of releasing her, he pulled her closer to him.

His mouth found her ear and he nibbled at the lobe. "Then you think you can ignore such outbursts in the future?" His voice was soft and, as she could barely hear him she leaned closer, unabashedly enjoying his nearness. He put a hand under her chin and turned her face to his.

For an endless moment they gazed deep into each other's eyes before Lord Umber brought his mouth down on hers and kissed her passionately.

"My darling Felicia," he murmured. "When will you marry me?"

Felicia felt so exquisite a joy envelop her that she was unable to do anything more than clasp her hands around his neck and bring his lips to hers again. A long time passed before she finally broke from her lover's embrace.

"Maybe I would prefer a house in Richmond," she said

mischievously. "With servants . . . and pin money . . . and . . ."

"Nay, my brazen hussy," Lord Umber broke in. " 'Tis marriage or nothing I propose this time."

"Then you force me to accept."

Mary Stewart

"Mary Stewart is magic" is the way Anthony Boucher *puts it. Each and every one of her novels is a kind of enchantment, a spellbinding experience that has won acclaim from the critics, millions of fans, and a permanent place at the top.*

☐	AIRS ABOVE THE GROUND	23868-7	$1.95
☐	THE CRYSTAL CAVE	23315-4	$1.95
☐	THE GABRIEL HOUNDS	23946-2	$1.95
☐	THE HOLLOW HILLS	23316-2	$1.95
☐	THE IVY TREE	23251-4	$1.75
☐	MADAM, WILL YOU TALK	23250-6	$1.75
☐	THE MOON-SPINNERS	23073-2	$1.75
☐	MY BROTHER MICHAEL	22974-2	$1.75
☐	NINE COACHES WAITING	23121-6	$1.75
☐	THIS ROUGH MAGIC	22846-0	$1.75
☐	THUNDER ON THE RIGHT	23100-3	$1.75
☐	TOUCH NOT THE CAT	23201-8	$1.95

Buy them at your local bookstores or use this handy coupon for ordering:

FAWCETT BOOKS GROUP
P.O. Box C730, 524 Myrtle Ave., Pratt Station, Brooklyn, N.Y. 11205

Please send me the books I have checked above. Orders for less than 5 books must include 75¢ for the first book and 25¢ for each additional book to cover mailing and handling. I enclose $_____ in check or money order.

Name_____
Address_____
City_____State/Zip_____

Please allow 4 to 5 weeks for delivery.